World's Dirtiest Jokes

Eat Your Spinach!

What do spinach and anal sex have in common?

If you were forced to have it as a kid, you'll hate it as an adult.

Millenial Workers

A man was warned repeatedly about hiring lazy, know-it-all, crybaby millenials to work in his factory. But he remembered when he was young and just starting out, so he wanted to give them a chance.

One morning, one of his tattooed millenials knocked on his office door.

"Yes?" he said.

"Boss, I have a problem," she said.

"What is it?" the boss asked.

"Well, I don't think it's appropriate that we test our products on animals. It's cruel."

"I realize your generation is very sensitive to these things," the boss said thoughtfully. "But we have to ensure our products are safe before we sell them to consumers. Shampoo companies test on animals, cosmetic companies test on animals. It's unfortunate for the animals, I admit, but it's a very common practice."

"But Boss, we make dildoes!" she exclaimed.

The Birth

A pregnant woman is about to give birth. The doctor has her on the delivery table, legs up in the stirrups. Suddenly, he sees the top of a head push through.

Then the baby pops its head out and says to the doctor, "Are you my dad?"

The doctor says, "No, I am your doctor."

With that, the baby pops right back inside.

"Damn!" says the doctor.

A short while later he sees the head push through again.

"Are you my dad?" asks the baby.

"No, I am your doctor," he replies.

Once again the baby vanishes back into his mother's womb.

The doctor turns to a nurse and says, "Nurse, get that baby's father in here right away – we may have a situation on our hands!"

Moments later the baby's father is in the delivery room, and the baby's head once again pops out.

"Are you my dad?" the baby asks of the father.

The father replies, "Yes, little baby, I am your father!"

The baby then reaches up and begins poking his father in the forehead with his index finger.

"How do you like it?"

The Car Ride

Little Sarah was riding in the car with her mother on her way to school when suddenly a huge dildo flew right onto the windshield, landed with a thump, and bounced off.

Little Sarah asked, "Mom, what was that?"

Her mother blushed, not wanting to explain the awkward situation to her young daughter, and said, "Um... it was an insect."

Sarah turned to look at the road behind them, "Damn, it had a really big dick!"

Doctor's Orders

A woman had gained some weight and went to see the doctor to see if he could help.

The doctor advised the woman, "Don't eat anything fatty."

She asked, "No bacon or sausages or burgers or anything?"

He said, "No, fatty, just don't eat anything."

Fool Me Twice?

Why don't black people go on cruises?

They already fell for that shit once before.

Erectile Dysfunction

A man told his doctor he had trouble getting an erection with his wife and she was getting frustrated.

The Doc checked the man's blood pressure and other vitals, then after a thorough examination, said he wanted to check with the Wife.

He took her to another examination room and asked her to disrobe. Then he told her to turn all the way around slowly.

She did as instructed.

He then told her to raise her arms above her head, then bend over, touch her toes and cough.

Finally he said, "OK, good. You can get dressed now and I will go talk to your husband."

The doctor went back to the other examination room and said to the Husband, "Well, Bill, you can relax, there is nothing wrong with you. I couldn't get an erection either."

Malpractice

While doing a vasectomy, the doctor slipped and cut off one of the man's balls. To avoid a huge malpractice suit, he decided to replace the missing testicle with a pickled onion. Several weeks later, the patient returned for a checkup.

"How's your sex life?" asked the doctor.

"Pretty good," the man said, to the doctor's obvious relief.

But then the patient added, "I've had some strange side effects that are causing serious problems."

"What's that?" the doctor asked anxiously.

"Well, every time I urinate, my eyes water."

"Hmm," said the doctor, thoughtfully.

"That's not all," continued the patient. "When my wife does me orally, she gets heartburn."

"Hmm," said the doctor, as his face reddened.

"It gets worse, Doc. Now, every time I pass a hamburger stand, I get an erection!"

The Postal Worker

John went to an interview for a job in the United States Postal Service.

The interviewer introduced himself, reviewed John's background on his resume, and said, "It says here you served in the military?"

"Yes," John said, "I was in Afghanistan for two years."

The interviewer nodded and said, "According to Federal hiring regulations, that will give you five extra points towards employment."

The interviewer continued, "Are you disabled in any way?"

John shook his head sadly and said, "Yes. A bomb exploded near me and I lost both of my testicles."

The interviewer looked at him sympathetically and said, "That's another five points. Finally, are you allergic to anything?"

John replied, "Yes, I am: coffee."

The interviewer looked across the desk, stuck out his hand, and said, "Congratulations, John, and welcome to the US Postal Service."

"Fantastic!" John said. "When do I start?"

"Well, our normal hours are from 8:00 am To 4:00 pm. But you can start tomorrow and just come in every day at 10:00 am."

John was puzzled, "If the work hours are from 8:00 am to 4:00 pm, why do you want me to start at 10:00 am? Is this a part-time job?"

"No, no, this is a government job," the interviewer said, "For the first two hours, we just stand around drinking coffee and scratching our balls. No point in you coming in for that."

Cute Little Girl

A young family moved into a new neighborhood. Their house was one of the first built, and it sat next to a vacant lot. One day, a construction crew turned up to start building a house on the empty lot.

The young family's 5-year-old daughter naturally took an interest in all the activity going on next door and spent much of each day observing the workers. Eventually the construction crew adopted her as a kind of project mascot.

They chatted with her, let her sit with them while they had coffee and lunch breaks, and gave her little jobs to do here and there to make her feel important. At the end of the first week, they even presented her with a pay envelope containing ten dollars.

The little girl took this home to her mother who suggested that she take her ten dollars "pay" she'd received to the bank the next day to start a savings account. When the girl and her mom got to the bank, the teller was equally impressed and asked the little girl how she had come by her very own paycheck at such a young age.

The little girl proudly replied: "I worked last week with a real construction crew building the new house next door to us."

"Oh my goodness gracious," said the teller, smiling down at the cute little girl, "and will you be working on the house again this week, too?"

The little girl replied, "I will if those lazy assholes ever deliver the fucking sheetrock."

The Dark Woods

A child molester and a little boy are walking in the woods at night, holding hands. The child molester and the little boy keep walking further and further, and it's getting darker and darker, and they're going deeper and deeper into the woods.

The little boy looks up at the child molester, his little hand gripping the older man's hand tightly, and says, "Gee, mister, I'm getting scared."

And the child molester looks down at him and says, "You think you're scared, kid? I have to walk out of here alone."

The Tolerant Girl

A little girl was water the flowers in the garden when she spied two spiders mating. "Daddy, what are those two spiders doing?" she asked.

"They're mating," her father replied.

"What do you call the spider on top, Daddy?" she asked.

"That's a daddy long legs," her father answered.

"So, the other one is a mommy long legs?" the little girl asked innocently.

"No," her father replied. "Both of them are daddy long legs."

The little girl thought for a moment, then took her foot and stomped them flat. "Well, we're not having any of *THAT* shit in our garden."

The Date

A young man and his date were parked on a back road some distance from town. They were about to have sex when the girl stopped.

"I really should have mentioned this earlier, but I'm actually a hooker and I charge $200 for sex."

The man reluctantly paid her, and they did their thing. After they were done, the man just sat in the driver's seat looking out the window.

"Why aren't we going anywhere?" asked the girl as she pulled her dress back on.

"Well, I should have mentioned this before, but I'm actually an Uber driver, and the fare back to town is $250."

The Playground

Little Jenny came home from school with a smile on her face, and told her mother, "Nathan Brown showed me his weenie today at the playground!"

Before the mother could raise a concern, Jenny went on to say, "It reminded me of a peanut."

Suppressing a smile, Jenny's mom asked, "Really small, was it?"

Jenny replied, "No, it tasted really salty."

The Examination

A man is sitting in the exam room in his doctor's office. The doctor puts his stethoscope down and says, "I'm afraid you're going to have to stop masturbating."

"I don't understand, doc," the patient says. "Why?"

"Because," the doctor says, "I'm trying to examine you."

The Medical Visit

A beautiful young woman walks into a doctor's office and the doctor is bowled over by how stunningly gorgeous she is. He immediately abandons all pretext of professionalism.

He guides her into an exam room and tells her to take off her dress. He sees her standing there just in her bra and panties, looking like a model.

The doctor places his hands on her breasts over her bra and starts to squeeze and massage her perky breasts.

"Do you know what I am doing?" asks the doctor as he eyes her voluptuous body.

"Yes, checking for breast cancer," she replies.

He then tells her to take off her bra and panties, and she obeys. The Doctor can't believe his luck – the most beautiful woman he has ever seen is now naked in his exam room.

The doctor begins rubbing her thighs and asks, "Do you know what I am doing now?"

She replies, "Yes, checking for abnormalities."

The Doctor is overwhelmed with passion. He tells her to bend over the exam table, gets behind her, and starts to have sex with her.

He pants, "Do you know what I'm doing now?"

"Yes," she replies. "Getting herpes. That's why I'm here."

The Pharmacist

The pharmacist asks his junior assistant to watch the counter while he takes a break. When he returns, he sees a man standing by the wall in visible discomfort.

He asks his assistant, "What's with that guy over there by the wall?"

The assistant says, "Well, he came in here to get something for his cough. I couldn't find the cough syrup, so I gave him an entire bottle of laxatives."

"You idiot! You can't treat a cough with laxatives!"

"Oh yeah? Look at him, he's afraid to cough!"

Marriage Vows

Three couples are trying to get married at the same church: a young couple, a middle-aged couple, and an elderly couple. All three couples meet with the priest and discuss when they can get married.

After discussing the process and requirements, the priest closes with a prayer. But before any of them can leave, he warns them, "If you wish to get married in my church, you must all go one month without having sex," says the priest.

One month later, the three couples return to the church and talk to the priest. He asks the elderly couple, "Have you completed the month with sex?"

"Yes we have, it was easy," replies the elderly couple.

"How about you?" he asks the middle-aged couple.

"It was hard, but we didn't have sex for the whole month," they respond.

"And how about you two?" He asks the young couple.

"No, we couldn't do it," responds the boyfriend.

"Tell me why," says the priest, shaking his head in disappointment.

"Well, my girlfriend had a can of corn in her hand and she accidentally dropped it. She bent over to pick it up and that's when it happened."

The priest then tells them, "I'm sorry, but with your lack of self-control, you're not welcome in my church."

"We're not welcome in the supermarket, either," says the boyfriend.

Mother's Wisdom

A mother is in the kitchen one day, preparing dinner for the family.

Her young daughter walks in and asks her, "Mommy, where do babies come from?"

The mother thinks for a while before deciding to be honest with her daughter.

She says, "Well, honey, Mommy and Daddy fall in love and get married. One night they go into their bedroom, they kiss and hug, and then they have sex."

The daughter looks confused, so the mother says, "That means that Daddy puts his penis between Mommy's legs. That's how you get a baby."

The daughter thinks for a moment and then seems to understand.

Then she looks up at her mother says, "I think I get it. But the other night when I came into your room, you had Daddy's penis in your mouth. What do you get when you do that?"

The mother replies, "Jewelry, my dear. Jewelry."

Dear Old Grandpa

I'll never forget my Grandfather's last words to me just before he died.

"Are you still holding the ladder?"

New Cookbook

For my birthday, my friend bought me a book called 'Road Kill Recipes'.

As luck would have it, the next day I came across some road kill, so I cooked it according to one of the recipes in the book. It was delicious!

I'm just not sure what I should do with the bike.

Cultural Differences

What is the difference between American teenage girls and Muslim teenage girls?

American teenage girls get stoned before they have sex.

The Maid

One day a Mexican maid announced to her boss, a pretty blonde wife, that she was quitting.

She asked her why, and the young maid replied, "Because I'm in the family way."

The wife was shocked to hear this, because the young maid was single, only eighteen years old, and lived in a room in their house with them. She'd never seen the maid with a boyfriend.

The wife asked who it was, and the maid replied, "Your husband and your son."

The wife was horrified to hear this. "My husband and my son?!?" she gasped. She demanded an explanation from the maid.

"Well," the maid explained, "I go to the library to clean it and your husband say, 'You are in the way'. I go to the living room to clean and your son say, 'You are in the way'."

The Mexican maid looked at the wife sadly and said, "So I'm in the family way and I quit."

Big Words

Guy in Arkansas comes home to find two suitcases packed on his front porch.

"What's goin' on honey?" he asks his wife.

"I'm leaving you!" she replies.

"But why?"

"I've just discovered that you're a child molesting pedophile!"

"Whooaahh... them's big words for a 9 year old!"

Medical Problem

A man says to his doctor, "You gotta help me, doc!"

The doctor says, "What's your problem?"

The guy replies, "Every morning I wake up with my 'morning flagpole', so I give the missus a quick one, then go to work. On the way to work, I car pool with the next door neighbor's wife, who gives me a blow job during the ride to work."

The doctor raises his eyebrows.

The man continues, "Once I get to work, I do some work, but after about two hours, I go into the photocopy room and have
it off with the one of the young office girls. At lunch I take my secretary out to a hotel and give her a good bonking. Later in the afternoon, I give it to the boss's wife, long and hard."

The doctor's mouth falls open.

The man continues, "Then I go home and slip the maid a few inches, and then at night I give the missus another screw."

"Oh, I see," said the doctor, trying to maintain his composure. "But what exactly is your problem?"

The man says, "Well, it hurts when I masturbate."

The Explorers

Three explorers representing North America are traveling through the Amazon on a joint mission to search for diamond deposits. The team consists of a Canadian, an American, and a Mexican. The three of them have a less-than-friendly rivalry and are always looking for ways to demonstrate the superiority of their home country.

Suddenly, a spear-wielding tribe surrounds them in the jungle. The three explorers have their hands tied behind their backs and are led deep into the jungle to the tribe's village.

The explorers, having heard stories of blood-thirsty cannibals in the Amazonian jungle, beg for their lives.

The tribe's chief announces that he will mercifully free the men, but each man will be whipped ten times for trespassing onto tribal lands.

The chief of the tribe says to the Canadian, "What do you want us to put on your back for your whipping?"

The Canadian replies, "I will take some of my great Canadian maple syrup!"

So the tribe puts his syrup on his back, and a large member of the tribe whips him ten times.

When he is finished, the Canadian has huge welts on his back and is in so much pain that he can hardly move.

The tribe hauls the sobbing Canadian away, and the chief says to the Mexican, "And what do you want on your back?"

The Mexican eyes the Canadian with disdain, smirks at the American, and bravely says, "I will take nothing!"

The Mexican stands still and takes his whipping without flinching.

Finally, the tribe asks the American, "And what will you take on your back?"

The American replies, "I'll take the Mexican."

Street Business

Two hookers were on a street corner. The night was young and the sun hadn't gone down yet, so they started discussing business.

One of the hookers said, "Yep, it's gonna be a good night, I smell cock in the air."

The other hooker looked at her and said, "No, no. I just burped."

Profitable Marriage

On their wedding night, the virginal young bride shyly approached her new husband and asked for $20 for their first lovemaking encounter.

He thought it was highly unusual, but in his highly aroused state, her husband readily agreed.

This scenario was repeated each time they made love. For more than 40 years, he thought that it was a cute way for her to afford new clothes and other incidentals that she needed.

Arriving home around noon one day, she was surprised to find her husband in a very drunken state. During the next few minutes, he explained that his employer was going through a process of corporate downsizing, and he had been fired.

He sobbed that it was unlikely that, at the age of 59, he'd be able to find another position that paid anywhere near what he'd been earning, and therefore, they were financially ruined.

Calmly, his wife handed him a bank book which showed more than forty years of steady deposits and interest totaling nearly $1 million.

Then she showed him the online statement from her brokerage that showed an account containing stocks and bonds valued at over $2 million.

She explained that for the decades she had 'charged' him for sex, she had saved all the money he'd ever given her and these holdings had multiplied.

Faced with evidence of cash and investments worth over $3 million that saves him from ruin, her husband was so

astounded he could barely speak, but his face turned bright red and he pounded his fists on the table.

"What's the matter, honey?" his wife asked.

He finally he found his voice and blurted out, "If I'd had any idea what you were doing, I would have given you all my business!"

Free Sex!

A gas station in Mississippi was trying to increase its sales, so the owner put up a sign saying, "Free Sex with Fill-Up".

Soon a local redneck pulled in, filled his tank, and then asked for his free sex.

The owner told him to pick a number from 1 to 10, and if he guessed correctly, he would get his free sex.

The redneck then guessed 8, and the proprietor said, "You were close. The number was 7. Sorry, no sex this time."

A week later, the same redneck, along with a buddy, Bubba, pulled in for a fill-up. Again he asked for his free sex.

The proprietor gave him the same story, and asked him to guess the correct number. The redneck guessed 2 this time. Again the proprietor said, "Sorry, it was 3. You were close, but no free sex this time."

As they were driving away, the redneck said to his buddy, "I think that game is rigged and he doesn't really give away free sex.

Bubba replied, "No it ain't, Billy Ray. It ain't rigged ---- my wife won twice last week."

Redneck Geneology

Two fellows from Alabama were sitting around talking one afternoon.

After a while the first fellow says to the second, "If'n I was to sneak over to your trailer Saturday and make love to your wife while you was off huntin', and she got pregnant and had a baby, would that make us kin?"

The second fellow crooked his head sideways for a minute, scratched his head, and squinted his eyes thinking real hard about the question.

Finally, he says, "Well, I don't know if it would make us kin, but it sure would make us even."

Interview Test

Bubba applied for an engineering position at a Lake Charles oil refinery. A black man applied for the same job and because both applicants had the same qualifications, they were both asked to take a test by the manager.

Upon completion of the test, both men only missed one of the questions. The manager went to Bubba and said: "Thank you for your interest, but we've decided to give the black man the job."

Bubba asked: "And why are you giving him the job? We both got nine questions correct. This being Louisiana, and me being white, I should get the job!"

The manager said: "We have made our decision not on the correct answers, but rather on the one question that you both missed."

Bubba then asked: "And just how would one incorrect answer be better than the other?"

The manager replied: "Bubba, its like this. On question #4, the black man answered, 'I don't know.'"

"You put down, 'Neither do I.'"

The Pill

A lady goes to the doctor and complains that her husband is losing interest in sex. The doctor gives her a pill, but warns her that it's still experimental. He tells her to slip it into his mashed potatoes at dinner. So that night, she does just that.

About a week later, she's back at the doctor, and says, "Doc, the pill worked great! I put it in the potatoes like you said. Not even five minutes later, he jumped up, raked all the food and dishes onto the floor, grabbed me, ripped all my clothes off, and ravaged me right there on the table!"

The doctor says, "Oh, gosh, I'm sorry, we didn't realize the pill was that strong! The drug company will be glad to pay for any damages."

"Nah," she says, "That's okay. We're never going back to that restaurant anyway."

Newlyweds

A newly-married couple were in the bathroom getting ready for work when the husband looked at his wife and said, "I gotta have you!"

He backed her up against the bathroom door, pulled down her panties, and ravaged her. He knew he was doing great because she screamed and wiggled more than she ever had before.

When he was finished, he started putting his clothes back on and when he noticed his wife still writhing against the door.

He smiled and said, "That was the best, honey. You've never moved like that before! You didn't hurt yourself, did you?"

And his wife replied, "No, no. I'll be okay once I can get this doorknob out of my ass."

Medical Professionalism

Doctor Dave had sex with one of his patients and felt guilty about it all day long. No matter how much he tried to forget about it, he couldn't. The guilt and sense of betrayal was overwhelming.

But every once in a while, he'd hear an internal, reassuring voice that said, "Dave, don't worry about it. You're not the first doctor to sleep with one of their patients and you won't be the last. And you're single. Just let it go."

But invariably the other voice would bring him back to reality, whispering, "Dave, you're a vet..."

The Girl's Lesson

The Dean of Girls at an exclusive girls' school was lecturing her students on sexual morality.

"We live today in very difficult times for young people. In moments of temptation," she said, "Ask yourself just one question: Is an hour of pleasure worth a lifetime of shame?"

A young girl rose in the back of the room and said shyly, "Excuse me, but how do you make it last an hour?"

Moving to Vegas

A husband comes home to find his wife with her suitcases packed in the living room.

"Where the hell do you think you're going?" he demanded.

"I'm going to Las Vegas. You can earn $400 for a blow job there, and I figured that I might as well earn money for what I do to you free."

The husband thinks for a moment, goes upstairs and comes back down with his suitcase packed as well.

"Where do you think you going?" the wife asks.

"I'm coming with you; I want to see how you survive on $800 a year!"

The Helpful Child

A little boy walked in on his dad masturbating. Never having seeing his father in such a delicate situation, he asked, shocked, "Dad, what are you doing?"

His dad replied, without ceasing, "Don't worry son, you're going to do it soon."

"Really? Why, Dad?" asked the kid.

"Well, my arm is getting tired..."

Kentucky Hang-glider

Here in Kentucky, you don't see too many people hang-gliding. After seeing one on TV, Bubba decided to save up and get a hang-glider for himself. He takes it to the highest mountain, and after struggling to the top, he gets ready to take flight. He takes off running and reaches the edge, and into the wind he goes!

Meanwhile, Maw and Paw Hicks were sittin' on the porch swing talkin' bout the good ol' days when Maw spots the biggest bird she ever seen!

"Look at the size of that bird, Paw!" she exclaims.

Paw raises up, "Git my gun, Maw."

She runs into the house, brings out his pump shotgun. He takes careful aim. BANG...BANG.....BANG.....BANG! The monster size bird continues to sail silently over the tree tops.

"I think ya missed him, Paw," she says.

"Yeah, but at least he let go of Bubba."

Anatomy Lesson

A little boy comes home from school and asks his father, "Dad, what does a vagina look like?"

The father thinks for a minute and says "Well, son, before sex a vagina looks like a beautiful and blossoming rose, with soft velvet petals and lovely fragrances."

"Wow," says the son. "But what about after sex?"

The father responds, "have you ever seen a bulldog eating mayonnaise?"

Sex Education

A little girl and her mother were walking through the park one day when they saw two teenagers having sex on a bench.

The little girl says, "Mommy what are they doing?"

The mother hesitates then quickly replies, "Ummm... they are making cakes. Now come on, we'll go to the zoo."

At the zoo, the little girl sees two monkeys having sex. Again she asks her mother "What are they doing?"

And her mother, unable to come up with a suitable response, says, "They're making cakes. That's it, we're going home"

The next day the girl says to her mother, "Mommy, you and Daddy were making cakes in the living room last night, weren't you?"

Shocked, the Mother says, "What? How do you know?"

She says, "Because I licked the icing off the sofa."

Tha's Racis'!

What did the black woman get for having an abortion?

500 bucks from CrimeStoppers.

Women's Work

Why does a woman have arms?

Because without arms it would take her hours to lick the bathroom clean.

A Family Affair

A boy walks into the bathroom when his father is taking a shower.

Curious, he asks his father, "What's that big hairy thing between your legs?"

The dad replies, "Your sister's head."

Mexican Shortage

Why were there only two thousand Mexicans at the battle of the Alamo?

Because they only had two trucks.

Lost Little Girl

So a guy is walking through the woods and comes upon a little girl crying by herself, all alone.

He says to her, "Aww, what's wrong, little girl?"

The girl says tearfully, "My dad and I were out walking the dog and the dog chased a duck into the lake and didn't come out. My dad went in after him and he hasn't come out either."

The man says, "Wow, this really isn't your day," as he unzips his pants.

The Comatose Patient

After a routine operation, a woman slipped into a coma unexpectedly and unexplainably. The doctors were at a loss. Having tried everything, the doctors were out of ideas and told her despondent husband that his wife was unlikely to ever recover.

One day, when the nurse was giving her a sponge bath, the patient's heartbeat began to speed up and she began to move slightly. The nurse discovered that the woman seemed to respond when she touched her inner thigh.

The doctors called her husband and explained the experience the nurse had, and told him that they think sexual stimulation might bring her out of the coma. The husband drove to the hospital immediately.

The doctor said to the husband, "We will leave the room, but we suggest you try to engage in oral sex with your wife and see if she responds."

The husband agreed, and everyone else left the room. About 10 minutes passed, and the husband came out of the room with a sad look on his face.

"Well, how did it go?" asked the doctor.

"Not good... she's dead..." replied the husband sadly.

The doctor replied, "What?! Dead? How did that happen?"

"Well, she probably choked to death..."

Stolen Car

A man stumbles out of a bar, weaving unsteadily back and forth with a key in his hand.

A cop working the late night shift watching for drunk drivers sees him and asks, "Can I help you, sir?"

"Yeah, hossifer, somebody stole my car!"

The cop asks, "Where was your car the last time you saw it?"

The man waved his car key in the policeman's face, "It was at the end of this key!"

About this time, the cop looks down to see that the man's pants are unbuttoned and his member is being exhibited for all the world to see.

He asks the man, "Sir, are you aware that you are exposing yourself?"

The man looks down, eyes his dangling exposed member, and moans woefully, "Oh my God! They got my wife too!"

The Shot

A banker and a priest are out for a game of golf one afternoon. Unfortunately, the banker wasn't very good at golf, and every time he missed a shot would shout, "Shit, I missed!"

The game went on and after several outbursts from the banker, the priest could hold his tongue no longer.

"Don't swear like that," he told his friend, "or God will punish you".

The banker apologized, swore to quit cursing, and the game continued.

But as soon as he missed another shot, the banker shouted, "Shit, I missed!"

The priest shook his head.

The banker continued to do this every time he missed a shot for the next three holes.

The priest was starting to get really angry and said, "I must insist that you stop swearing this instant, otherwise God will hear you and punish you!"

Once again, his pleas made no difference as the banker missed an easy putt on the seventeenth green and shouted out "Shit, I missed!"

Suddenly the clouds parted and a bolt of lightning flew from the sky. The banker looked down, astonished: the lightning hit the priest and killed him instantly.

A booming voice was heard in the clouds, "Shit, I missed!"

Ski Trip

Charlie decided to go skiing with his buddy, Jack. They loaded up Jack's truck and headed north. After driving for a few hours, they got caught in a terrible blizzard. They pulled into a nearby farm and asked the attractive older lady who answered the door if they could spend the night.

"I realize it's terrible weather out there and I have this huge house all to myself, but I'm recently widowed," she explained, "I'm afraid the neighbors will talk if I let you stay in my house."

"Don't worry," Charlie said. "We'll be happy to sleep in the barn. And if the weather breaks, we'll be gone at first light."

The lady agreed, and the two men found their way to the barn and settled in for the night. Come morning, the weather had cleared, and they got on their way. They enjoyed a great weekend of skiing.

About nine months later, Charlie got an unexpected letter from an attorney. It took him a few minutes to figure it out, but he finally determined that it was from the attorney of that attractive widow he had met on the ski weekend.

He dropped in on his friend Jack and asked, "Jack, do you remember that good-looking old widow from the farm we stayed at on our ski holiday up North?"

"Yes, I do," Jack said with a sly smile.

"Did you happen to get up in the middle of the night, go up to the house, and pay her a visit?"

"Yes," Jack said, a little embarrassed about being found out, "I have to admit that I did. In fact, I had sex with her all night long."

"And did you happen to use my name instead of telling her

your name?"

Jack's face turned red and he said, "Yeah, sorry, buddy. I'm afraid I did. I didn't want my wife to ever find out. Why do you ask?"

"She just died and left me everything."

The Business Trip

A father came home from a long business trip to find his son with a brand new mobile phone.

"Where did you get the money for the phone?" he demanded.

"Easy, Dad," the boy replied. "I earned it hiking."

"Hiking? You've earned money *hiking*? Come on," the father said. "Tell me the truth."

"That is the truth," the boy replied. "Every night you were gone, that nice black man from next door would come over to see Mom. He'd give me a $20 bill and tell me to take a hike!"

The Country Doctor

A young doctor had moved out to a small rural community to replace the old doctor who was retiring. The old doctor suggested the young one accompany him on his rounds so the community could become used to a new doctor.

At the first house a woman complained, "I've been a little sick to my stomach."

The old doctor said, "Well, you've probably been overdoing the fresh fruit. Why don't you cut back on the amount you've been eating and see if that does the trick?"

As they left the young doctor said, "You didn't even examine that woman. How'd you come to your diagnosis so quickly?"

"I didn't have to. You noticed I dropped my stethoscope on the floor in there? When I bent over to pick it up, I noticed a half dozen banana peels in the trash. That was what was probably making her sick."

"Hmmm," the young doctor said, "Pretty clever. I think I'll try that at the next house."

Arriving at the next house, they spent several minutes talking with a younger woman. She complained that she just didn't have the energy she once did.

"I'm feeling terribly run down lately," se said.

"You've probably been doing too much extra work for the church," the young doctor told her. "Perhaps you should cut back a bit and see if that helps."

As they left, the old doctor said, "Your diagnosis is almost certainly correct, but how did you arrive at it?

"Well, just like you did at the last house, I dropped my stethoscope and when I bent down to retrieve it, I noticed the preacher under the bed."

The Experiment

A very shy guy goes into a bar and sees a beautiful woman sitting at the bar. After an hour of gathering up his courage, he finally goes over to her.

He asks, tentatively, "Um, would you mind if join you for a bit?"

She responds by yelling, at the top of her lungs, "No, I won't sleep with you tonight!"

Everyone in the bar is now staring at them. Naturally, the guy is hopelessly and completely embarrassed and he slinks back to his table.

After a few minutes, the woman walks over to him and apologizes.

She smiles at him and says, "I'm sorry if I embarrassed you. You see, I'm a graduate student in psychology and I'm studying how people respond to embarrassing situations."

He smiles back and responds, at the top of his lungs, "What do you mean $200?"

The Children

One day a man says to his wife, "Honey, I've never said anything before, but I need to know: All of our seven children are good-looking, intelligent kids, except Tyrone. Tyrone, well, Tyrone is not. I love him and all, but you gotta admit he's a pretty stupid, ugly kid. Does Tyrone have a different father than his siblings?"

The wife says, "Yes, I admit it: he does."

The husband gasps and says, "Who is his father?"

The wife responds, "You are."

Human Trafficking

A flight attendant sees a suspicious-looking couple on board, so she reports it to the Captain immediately.

"Sir, I think we have a case of human trafficking! There is a very pretty young female passenger on board. She looks quite frightened, and the man she is with is a fat old slob."

The captain responds, "Patricia, I've told you this before. This is Air Force One..."

The Atheist

A priest was on a flight when the passenger next to him sneezed.

"Bless you," the priest said kindly, even though the man hadn't bothered to cover his mouth or nose.

"You can't bless me," the man responded rudely. "I'm an atheist."

"An atheist? Well, what happens when you die?"

The atheist shrugged, "When I die, I become part of the Earth, and I grow into a beautiful tree."

The priest smiled, "That's lovely. I hope you do become a beautiful tree. And then we can chop you down, make paper, and print lovely Bibles out of you."

The Morgue

Two guys were working late in a morgue, when one guy said, "Hey man, there's a woman in there with a shrimp in her vagina!"

The other asked, "What is a shrimp doing a dead woman's vagina? I've gotta see this!"

Both of them went in the room with the woman, and they both looked closely.

Finally, the second man said, "You idiot, this ain't no shrimp, it's a clitoris."

And the other man replied, "Well, it tasted like shrimp to me."

The Good Wife

Earl and Bubba are quietly sitting in a boat fishing, chewing tobacco, and drinking beer when suddenly Bubba says, "Think I'm gonna divorce the wife... she ain't spoke to me in over 2 months."

Earl spits overboard, takes a long, slow sip of beer and says, "Better think it over... women like that are hard to find."

Helping the Homeless

I invited a young homeless man to come live with me and my wife for a while. He took a nice long bath and shaved while I went out and and bought some brand new clothes for him. Then I took him to a hair stylist for finishing touches. He looked quite presentable. He was very personable and seemed quite intelligent.

It wasn't long before I noticed my wife behaving strangely towards him. She seemed flirtatious. I began to suspect my wife had developed romantic feelings toward the man.

I spoke to the man privately and told him of my observations and suspicions. Then I asked him directly if he planned to romance my wife and run off with her.

"Absolutely not!" he insisted. "Not after everything you've done for me! I would never betray you like that!"

So I kicked him out of the house and I'm looking for a new young homeless man to live with us.

The Researcher

A Harvard researcher was studying linguistic dialects among rural African American populations in the deep south. The researcher drove down into an agricultural area known to be populated by generations of black farmers. The researcher felt quite out of place; it was very different from genteel Harvard yard.

As the researcher was driving down a quiet country lane, a rooster strayed out into the road. Whack! The rooster disappeared under the car in a cloud of feathers.

Shaken, the man pulled over. The rooster was dead under his car. The researcher, wearing his starched khakis and white button-down shirt with a Harvard tie, walked to the nearest farmhouse and rang the doorbell. An old black farmer appeared, eyeing the white man.

The researcher somewhat nervously said, "I think I killed your rooster, please allow me to replace him."

"Suit yourself," the farmer replied in a thick Southern drawl, "the hens are 'round back."

The Deserters

On the street just outside a military base, a soldier ran up to a nun. Out of breath, he asked, "Please, Sister, may I hide under your skirt? I'll explain later."

The nun agreed.

A moment later, two military policemen ran up and asked, "Sister, have you seen a soldier?"

The nun pointed off down the street and said, "He went that way."

After the MPs ran off, the soldier crawled out from under her skirt and said, "I can't thank you enough, sister. You see, I don't want to go to Syria."

The nun said, "I understand completely."

The soldier added, "I hope I'm not rude, but you have a great pair of legs!"

The nun replied, "If you had looked a little higher, you would have seen a great pair of balls, too. I don't want to go to Syria either."

The Business

A guy walks into a fancy restaurant and goes up to the bar. He asks to the bartender, "How much for a beer?"

The bartender replies, "One dollar."

The guy is completely amazed at the price and immediately orders a beer.

He then asks the bartender, "Well, then, just out of curiosity, how much for a New York sirloin, with side of mashed potatoes, and a salad, and an entire cheesecake for dessert?"

The bartender replies, "Three bucks."

The guy is stunned. He orders everything, and after he is done eating his meal, he says, "Wow, the food is amazing, especially at these prices. I really wish I could meet the owner of this place."

The bartender says "Oh, well, he's upstairs in his office with my wife".

The guy looks at the bartender, confused, and asks, "What is the owner doing upstairs in his office with your wife?"

The bartender says, "The same thing I'm doing to his business."

The Bet

A little old lady went to the Bank of America one day, carrying a bag of money. She insisted that she must speak with the CEO of the bank to open a savings account.

"It's a lot of money!" the old lady insisted.

After much hemming and hawing, the bank staff finally ushered her into their Chief Executive Officer's office. The bank CEO then asked her how much she would like to deposit.

She replied, "$165,000," and dumped the cash out of her bag onto his desk.

The CEO was, of course, curious as to how she came by all this cash, so he asked her, "Ma'am, I'm surprised you're carrying so much cash around. Where did you get this money?"

The old lady replied, "I make bets."

The CEO then asked, "Bets? You mean gambling? What kind of bets?"

The old woman said, "Well, for example, I'll bet you $25,000 that your balls are square."

"Ha!" laughed the CEO, "That's a stupid bet. You can never win that kind of bet!"

The old lady challenged, "So, would you like to take my bet?"

"Sure," said the CEO, "I'll bet $25,000 that my balls are not square!"

The little old lady then said, "Okay, but since there is a lot of money involved, may I bring my lawyer with me tomorrow at 10:00 am as a witness?"

"Sure!" replied the confident CEO.

That night, the CEO got a little nervous about the bet, wondering if the old lady had some kind of trick up her sleeve, and spent a long time in front of the mirror checking his balls, turning from side to side, again and again. He thoroughly checked them out until he was sure that there was absolutely no way his balls were square and he was certain he would win the bet. The next morning, at precisely 10:00 am, the little old lady appeared with her lawyer at the CEO's office.

She introduced the lawyer to the CEO and repeated the bet, "$25,000 says the president's balls are square!"

The CEO agreed with the bet again and the old lady asked him to drop his pants so they could all see. The CEO complied. The little old lady peered closely at his balls and then asked if she could feel them.

"Well, okay," said the CEO, "$25,000 is a lot of money, so I guess you should be absolutely sure."

Just then, the CEO noticed that the lawyer was quietly banging his head against the wall.

The CEO asked the old lady, "What the hell's the matter with your lawyer?"

She replied, "Nothing, except I bet him $100,000 that at 10:00 am today, I'd have the Bank of America's CEO's balls in my hand."

The Knife

Bill Clinton walks into a fancy restaurant with a gorgeous girl, young enough to be his granddaughter, on one arm and a loaf of bread under the other arm.

Donald Trump is standing at the bar. He eyes the young girl wearing a skin-tight dress and sky-high heels and he raises his drink to Bill in admiration. Then he notices the bread that Bill is carrying.

Trump says, "Hey Bill, what's the loaf of bread for?"

Bill smiled broadly at Donald, gives the girl a little pat on the butt, and says, "Whenever I get home after a night out with another woman, Hillary is waiting with a twelve-inch kitchen knife ready to kill me. But I hand her the bread and her instincts kick in -- and she makes me a sandwich instead."

The Ex-Presidents

Bill Clinton, Barack Obama, and Jimmy Carter, all three of the living Democratic Presidents, are flying back on a luxurious fuel-guzzling private jet from a conference where they all collected million-dollar fees to speak on the evils of capitalism. Jimmy Carter brought ten adorable young schoolgirls from his church choir to sing at the conference, and he insisted that they fly back on the top-of-the-line jet with the former Presidents.

As the plane is over the Atlantic, they encounter terrible turbulence, rocking and shaking the plane. Suddenly, one engine dies. Then the other engine dies. The plane begins to plummet toward the ocean below. The poor young girls on the plane begin to cry.

Jimmy Carter gets up to check with the pilots and returns with bad news.

"Gentlemen, we're going down, and there aren't enough parachutes on the plane for us and all the girls."

Barack Obama grabs a parachute and said, "Fuck the schoolgirls."

Bill Clinton looks at Barack and said, "Do you think there's time?"

The Presidential Library

Barack Obama was planning on installing a gigantic golden statue of himself in front of his new Presidential library in Chicago. He wanted it bigger than any statue every built of a Roman Emperor. He had his team draw up plans for an enormous gilded statue of himself that would dominate the city for centuries to come.

When it came time to build it, Obama's staff told him there were two contractors who wanted to build it: one white-owned business and one black-owned business.

"Give the contract to the black guy," Obama ordered.

"But sir!" his staff complained, "That's illegal."

Obama smiled and said, "Here's what we did when I was President: have the white guy bid first, and then show his bid to the black guy and tell him to come in $1 under. That way no one can say I'm unfair."

His staff followed orders, and they received a bid from the white-owned business for one million dollars for such a big job. The bid carefully detailed that they would need $500,000 for materials, $400,000 for labor, and $100,000 in payoffs to the local Chicago unions and Democratic politicians.

Obama's staff secretly sent the bid to the black-owned business. After a couple days, they received a response from the black-owned business, but instead of being $1 less than the white bid, it was just one line: three million dollars! Obama was shocked and demanded a meeting with the black owner.

When the black owner arrived, Obama said, "I want to give you the business, but the white bid was $1 million, and your bid is $3 million! How can you possible justify that? Explain to me how it could cost three times as much!"

The black contractor smiled and said, "It's simple: $1 million for you, $1 million for me, and $1 million to make whitey do the work for us!"

Man of the People

Donald Trump's approval ratings are in the toilet, and he's told by his political advisors that he needs to work on his image.

"Act like a normal American – go to a diner and order some chili," his political advisor tells him.

So Trump walks into a diner, cameras following his every move, and he walks up to the counter, hops on a stool, and orders a bowl a chili.

The waitress says that the man sitting next to him just ordered the last bowl of chili. That man was just sitting there, not eating the chili.

"Would you like a nice kale salad instead?" the waitress asks Trump.

Trump, aware the cameras are watching, declines.

After watching the man at the counter not eating his chili for a while, Trump asks him, "Are you going to eat that?"

The man replies, "No, you can have it if you want."

So Trump takes the bowl and starts eating, smiling for the cameras.

About halfway through the bowl, he's chewing when he feels a crunch. He looks down only to see half of a dead rat floating in the chili.

Horrified, he immediately throws it up, right back into the bowl.

The man at the counter looks at Trump and says, "Yeah, that's about as far as I got, too."

Presidential Daughters

After a hard day running the country, Donald Trump stopped over to see Barack Obama, and, as usual, Barack was lazily sitting on his couch.

Donald says, "How's it going, Barry? Seen how great the economy is now?"

Without getting up or even looking away from his TV, Barack says, "Whatever. Hey, will you run upstairs and get my slippers? My feet are freezing."

Donald shakes his head, "You're so lazy, Barry."

But Donald feels sorry for Barack, so he goes upstairs to get his slippers for him. Walking past a bedroom, Donald sees Barack's two teen daughters, Sasha and Malia, lying on the bed. It occurs to Donald that while he's had sex with models and porn stars, he's never had sex with two black sisters.

He stops in the doorway and says to them, "Your dad sent me up here to have sex with both of you."

Sasha looks up and says, "No way."

"Yeah," says Malia, "Prove it!"

Donald shouts downstairs, knowing Barack is too lazy to come up, "Barry, both of them?"

Barack shouts back from the couch, "Of course both of them, what's the point of just fucking one?"

The Deal

Early in their marriage, well before they achieved wealth and power, Barack and Michelle Obama were discussing ways to take over the country when suddenly the Devil appeared before them.

The Devil said, "I will give you money, power, and the ability to impose your will on others, but you must give me your immortal souls and work for the domination of Evil over the world and the oppression of all mankind."

Michelle and Barack quietly discussed it together and Barack replied, "So what's the catch?"

The Doctor

Michelle Obama was having some medical issues that were beyond the scope of her regular doctor, so her doctor referred her to a specialist.

"I should warn you," her doctor said, "the specialist is a man."

"Oh!" gasped Michelle.

"And he's white."

"No!" gasped Michelle, shaking her head.

"And he's a Republican," said her doctor.

"Oh no!" gasped Michelle, "Not that! Isn't there anyone else?"

Her doctor assured her that the specialist was the best: top of his field, very expensive, and he only treated private clients.

Michelle went to her appointment with some trepidation. She was shown into a large room at the specialist's office. His office was ornate, with a large Persian rug, an elaborate gilded desk, and bookcases full of leather-bound books instead of the normally austere examination room.

The nurse who showed her in asked Michelle to completely disrobe and put on a paper gown. Michelle complied.

Soon, the doctor came in, introduced himself, asked her a few perfunctory medical questions, and then asked her to stand and remove the paper gown.

Michelle reluctantly disrobed, shuddering to think she was naked in front of a white male Republican.

The doctor looked at her at said, "Mrs. Obama, please go over to that wall and lie on the floor under that window."

Michelle thought that was a strange request, but the doctor was highly recommended and had an impeccable reputation, so she complied, lying naked on the floor under the window for several minutes.

The doctor made some notes in the file.

"Now come and lie over here along this wall to the right of the bookcase," he said.

Michelle obeyed, stretching out naked next to the bookcase, and the specialist made some more notes.

"Lastly, come here to the middle of the room, and lie face-down on the floor, parallel to and in front of my desk, but about five feet away from it."

Again, Michelle obeyed, stretching out naked again, this time in the middle of the room as he said. The doctor shook his head, scratched his brow, and made some more notes in his file. He then walked over to Michelle and stood over her, looking down. He then turned around and slowly sat down on top of her, remaining there for almost a minute. Michelle just lay there, assuming there must be some medical justification for such an odd examination.

The specialist then stood up and told Michelle that she may get dressed. While she dressed, the doctor sat at his desk and continued to look at the file and make notes, but he said nothing to her. When she finished dressing, the doctor had still said nothing, and Michelle was getting a little worried about what might be wrong with her.

She finally asks, "Doctor, what have you been able to conclude might be causing all my symptoms? Have you figured out what's wrong with me?"

The doctor replied without looking up, "Oh, no, I have no idea what's wrong with you," and went back to taking notes.

So now Michelle was pissed off.

"Listen, Doctor," she said angrily, "You came highly recommended. You're the best in your field, so I didn't question your method of having me lie naked around your office even though I'm the former First Lady of the United States! Why did you have me perform such an unusual examination, even sitting on me, and then not tell me anything? Do I have some disease? Am I dying?"

The doctor put down his pen, closed his file, and looked down at Michelle over the top of his glasses with an exasperated sigh.

"No need to worry," he said. "I'm just thinking about getting a new brown leather sofa for this office, and I'm trying to figure out where in the room it would look best."

The Flight

Barack Obama was seated next to a little girl on an airplane trip back to Washington.

He turned to her with a smile and said, "It's your lucky day, young lady. I, Barack Hussein Obama, the greatest President America has ever had the pleasure of serving, shall talk with you during this flight."

The little girl, who had just opened her book, closed it slowly and said to the former President, "What would you like to talk about?"

"Oh, I don't know," said Obama, smiling benevolently down at the little girl. "How about the changes I should make to America as an ex-President?"

"OK," she says. "That could be an interesting topic. But let me ask you a question first. A horse, a cow, and a deer all eat pretty much the same stuff – mostly grass. Yet a deer excretes little pellets, while a cow turns out a flat patty, and a horse produces clumps of dried grass. Why do you suppose that is?"

Obama, visibly surprised by the little girl's intelligence, thinks about it for a second and finally says, "Hmmm, I have no idea."

To which the little girl replies, "Do you really feel qualified to change America when you don't know shit?"

The Exam

Bill Clinton was feeling poorly and had his staff schedule an appointment with his doctor. But when he got to his appointment, Clinton discovered that his old doctor had retired and was replaced by a drop-dead gorgeous redhead.

As she walks into the examining room, his jaw drops and his old horndog instincts kick in.

She looks at him, well-aware of his reputation, and says, "Yes, Mr. President, I know I'm young and good-looking. But I can assure you that I graduated top of my class and have excelled at my internship. I am absolutely qualified to diagnose any problem you might have. So, what are you in here for today?"

"Hillary says my dick tastes funny."

The Blessing

One day George, an atheist, was betting on the ponies. He was losing pretty badly when he noticed an old priest who had stepped out onto the track and blessed the forehead of one of the horses lining up for the 4th race.

Lo and behold, the horse, which was a very long shot, won the race.

George watched the priest closely in the next race. Sure enough, the priest step out onto the track as the horses lined up for the 5th race. The old priest placed his blessing on the forehead of one of the horses.

George made a beeline for the window and placed a small bet on the horse. Again, though another long shot, the horse won.

George collected his winnings and anxiously waited to see which horse the priest bestowed his blessing on for the 6th race. The priest showed up again on the track and blessed a horse.

George bet on it and he won!

George was elated. As the day went on, the priest continued blessing one of the horses and it always came in first.

George began to pull in some serious money and by the last race, he knew his wildest dreams were about to come true. He made a quick stop at the bank and withdrew every penny he owned, and then waited to see which horse the priest blessed.

True to his pattern, the priest stepped out onto the track before the last race and blessed not only the forehead, but the eyes, ears and hooves of one of the horses.

George eagerly placed his bet -- every cent he owned -- and watched with heart-pounding anticipation as they

announced the race. But his horse stumbled out of the gate, fell way behind, swerved badly across the track, before dropping dead halfway around the track. George was shocked!

He made his way to the track and when he found the priest, he demanded, "What happened, Father? All day long, you blessed horses and they won. But on the last race, you bless a horse and he not only loses, he drops dead! Now I've lost my life savings thanks to you!"

The priest nodded wisely and said, "That's the problem with you atheists. You can't tell the difference between a simple blessing and the Last Rites."

The Elevator

A beautiful young woman with large, perky breasts in a tight top and a short, tight skirt got into an elevator with a man. She leaned over to press the button for her floor and the man couldn't help admiring her body. The elevator started moving up, but, with a jolt, came to a stop between floors.

"Oh, that's just great!" the young woman said, "How long are we going to be stuck in here?"

"Dunno," the man replied, "maybe hours."

The elevator started to get warmer, and as she got hotter, the young woman started to unbutton her top a little more. The man couldn't help staring. Then she noticed his erection and gave him a little smile. After a few minutes, he had her naked and was drilling her against the wall.

They finished and she started to get dressed. She asked, "I've never seen you in here before, what department do you work in?"

"Oh, I don't work here," he answered, "I'm just here to fix the elevator."

The IRS

At the end of the tax year, the IRS office sent an inspector to audit the books of a local hospital.

While the IRS agent was checking the books, he turned to the Chief Financial Officer of the hospital and said, "I notice you buy a lot of bandages. What do you do with the end of the roll when there's too little left to be of any use?"

"Good question," noted the CFO. "We save them up and send them back to the bandage company and, every once in a while, they send us a free roll."

"Oh," replied the auditor, somewhat disappointed that his unusual question had a practical answer. But on he went in his arrogant and obnoxious way.

"What do you do with the left over plaster after setting a cast on a patient?"

"Ah, yes," replied the CFO, realizing that the auditor was trying to trap him with an unanswerable question. "We save it and send it back to the manufacturer and every so often they will send us a free bag of plaster."

"I see," replied the auditor, thinking hard about how he could fluster the know-it-all CFO.

"Well," he went on, "what do you do with all the remains from the circumcision surgeries?"

"Here, too, we do not waste," answered the CFO. "What we do is save all the little foreskins and send them to the IRS office, and about once a year they send us a complete prick."

The President of Oz

Presidents Trump, Clinton, and Obama are flying together on Air Force On when they are caught in a tornado, and off they spin to OZ. After great difficulty, they finally make it down the yellow brick road to the Emerald City and come before the Great Wizard.

"WHAT BRINGS YOU BEFORE THE GREAT AND POWERFUL WIZARD OF OZ? WHAT DO YOU WANT?"

Barack Obama steps forward timidly, "My foreign policy was pretty bad. I had a terrible time getting bullied by Iran and Syria and Russia and Libya, so I've come for some courage."

"NO PROBLEM!" says the Wizard, "WHO IS NEXT?"

Donald Trump steps forward, "Well, this job is harder than I thought. I... I think I need a brain. A yuge brain!"

"DONE" says the Wizard.

"WHO COMES NEXT BEFORE THE GREAT AND POWERFUL OZ?"

Then there is a great silence in the hall. Bill Clinton is just standing there, looking around, but doesn't say a word.

Irritated, the Wizard finally asks, "WHAT BRINGS YOU TO THE EMERALD CITY?"

Bill replies, "Is Dorothy around?"

Politics

A little boy goes to his father and asks, "Dad, what is politics?"

The dad says, "Well son, let me try to explain it this way: I'm the breadwinner of the family, so let's call me capitalism. Your mother, she's the administrator of the money, so we'll call her the government. We're here to take care of your needs, so we'll call you the people."

The boy nodded.

His father continued, "The nanny, we'll consider her the working class. And your baby brother, we'll call him the future. Now, think about that and see if that makes sense."

The little boy nodded again, and went off to bed thinking about what dad had said.

Later that night, he hears his baby brother crying, so he gets up to check on him. He finds that the baby has soiled his diaper.

The little boy goes to his parents' room and finds his mother sound asleep. Not wanting to wake her, he goes to the nanny's room.

Finding the door locked, he peeks in the keyhole and sees his father in bed with the nanny. He gives up and goes back to bed.

The next morning, the little boy says to his father, "Dad, I think I understand the concept of politics now."

The father says, "Good son, tell me in your own words what you think politics is all about."

The little boy replies, "Well, while capitalism is screwing the working class, the government is sound asleep, the people are being ignored, and the future is in deep shit."

The Carpenter's Son

St. Peter stood at the Pearly Gates, waiting for the incoming, and he needed to use the restroom. He saw Jesus walking by and caught his attention.

"Jesus, could you mind the gate while I go take a leak?"

"Sure," replied Jesus. "What do I have to do?"

"Just find out about the people who arrive. Ask about their background, their family, and their lives. Then decide if they deserve entry into Heaven."

"Sounds easy enough," Jesus shrugged.

So Jesus waited at the gates while St. Peter went off on his errand. The first person to approach the gates was a wrinkled old man. Jesus summoned him to a chair in front of a Heavenly desk and sat across from him.

Jesus peered at the old man and asked, "What was it you did for a living?"

The old man replied, "I was a carpenter."

Jesus remembered his own earthly existence and leaned forward and asked, "Did you have any family?"

"Yes, I had a son," the old man nodded, "but I lost him."

Jesus leaned forward some more.

"You lost your son? Can you tell me about him?"

"Well, he had holes in his hands and feet," the old man said tearfully.

Jesus leaned forward even more and whispered, "Father?"

The old man leaned forward and whispered, "Pinocchio?"

The Funeral

Muldoon lived alone in the Irish countryside with only a pet dog for company. One day, the poor dog died, and Muldoon went to the parish priest and asked, "Father, my dog is dead. Could ya' be saying' a mass for the poor creature?"

Father Patrick replied, "I'm afraid not; we cannot have services for an animal in the church. But there are some Baptists down the lane, and there's no tellin' what they believe. Maybe they'll do something for the creature."

Muldoon said, "I'll go right away Father. Do ya' think $5,000 is enough to donate to them for the service?"

Father Patrick exclaimed, "Sweet Mary, Mother of Jesus! Why didn't ya tell me the dog was Catholic?"

The Herdsman

An American soldier in Afghanistan was passing a small village on patrol when he came across a local herdsman with his dog and livestock.

"Is that your dog?" the soldier asked.

The Muslim replied, "Yes, praise be to Allah."

"Mind if I talk to him?"

The Muslim herdsman looked at the soldier as if he was crazy and said, "Holy Mohammed! Don't you Americans know dogs can't talk?"

The soldier shrugged, "So what's the harm? May I try?"

The herdsman nodded.

The Cowboy said to the dog, "Howdy!"

The dog replied, in perfect English, "Hello."

The herdsman's eyes popped wide open.

The soldier continued, "Is this your master?"

"Yep, he sure is," the dog said.

"Does he treat you alright?"

"Sure does. Every day he takes me for a walk, he feeds me all kinds of great food, and once a week he takes me to the lake to play."

The herdsman was completely dumbfounded.

The soldier said to the herdsman, "Is that your donkey over there?"

"Yes."

"Do you mind if I talk to him, too?"

The herdsman replied, "I know the dog spoke to you, but I know for a fact that donkeys can't talk."

"Well, then, what would it hurt?"

"Go right ahead," the herdsman said.

The soldier said to the donkey, "Hello."

The donkey replied, in flawless English, "Hello."

The herdsman stood there with his jaw wide open.

The soldier asked, "Is that your owner?"

"Yup, sure is."

"He treat you okay?"

"Sure, he rides me every day, brushes me down at the end of the day, and he keeps me in the barn away from the elements," said the donkey.

"Sounds good."

The soldier then asked the herdsman, "Are those your sheep over there?"

The herdsman is horrified and stammers, "Those sheep out there, they're nothing but a bunch of liars!"

Confession

Father O'Malley is hearing confessions one day when he suddenly feels an attack of the Hershey squirts coming on. He quickly calls the church janitor, Mr. Hennesy, over.

The priest begs the janitor to take his place hearing confessions while he runs for the men's room.

"Sorry Father, I wouldn't know what to do. I wouldn't know what to give for penance. How many Hail Mary's? How many Our Fathers?"

"It's very simple, my son. There's a book in here. Just look up the sin and it tells you the penance."

Hennesy reluctantly agrees to take the good father's place while the priest makes a dash for the toilet. He's a little nervous at first but it doesn't take long before he gets the hang of it.

He flips through the book and sees ten Hail Mary's for masturbation, five Our Fathers and five Hail Mary's for adultery. Pretty simple.

All goes well until a young woman enters the booth and confesses to giving her boss a blow job.

Hennesy flips through the pages. No blow jobs anywhere in the book. Hennesy is frantic and the father is still busy in the men's room. He needs to ask someone, anyone, what to do. He opens the confessional door a crack and he sees little Timmy O'Toole, an altar boy, waiting his turn to confess.

"Psst! Hey kid! What does Father O'Malley give for a blow job?"

Timmy smiles and answers, "Usually a Big Mac and a chocolate shake."

The Shipwreck

A Jew, a Muslim, a Catholic, and a Mormon are shipwrecked on a small desert island. They have very little food and water, and the situation is perilous.

The Muslim finds a corner of the beach, prostrates himself, and prays to Allah for succor.

The Mormon finds a different corner and prays fervently to God.

The Catholic heads for a palm tree, sits down, and begins reciting the rosary non-stop, her beads miraculously having survived the wreck.

The Jew continues hanging out by the shore, picking up a shell now and then, and occasionally skipping rocks.

After a little while, the Muslim, Mormon, and Catholic realize that the Jew's just idly staring off into the distance, whistling a little tune, instead of doing everything possible to get them saved.

They confront the Jew and say, "Hey, you jerk! We're all doing the best we can to get a little divine intervention here! How about you help us cover your base, eh?"

The Jew just smiles for a moment.

Then he says, "Well, every year for the past ten years on the first of next month, I've donated about $20,000 to the Jewish Federation."

The Catholic, outraged, replies, "So what? What does that have to do with anything?"

The Jew answers, "Don't worry. They'll find me."

The Miracle

An Irish priest is driving home from a night at his favorite bar. A police officer notices a car swerving all over the road and proceeds to pursue. The Irishman pulls over and the cop makes his way to the driver.

Checking the vehicle and noticing bottles over the floorboard, the Policeman asks, "Have you been drinking?"

"I don't know what you're on about, Officer. I had only just left church after giving praise to the Lord for his many blessings and miracles," said the Priest.

The policeman frowned, "Well then, what's in the bottles?"

"Water," the priest replied.

The Policeman reached in and grabbing a bottle, opened the top and was quickly overcome with the smell.

"This is wine!"

The Priest promptly shouted, "PRAISE THE LORD, HE'S DONE IT AGAIN!"

The Crucifixion

Jesus was hanging on the cross and calling out pitifully, "John! John!"

His apostle, John, tried to fight his way past the guards, but he couldn't get close enough to talk to Jesus.

After each attempt, Jesus cried out for him from high up on the cross, "John! John!"

Battered and bruised, on his sixth attempt, John finally made it to the base of the cross.

"Yes, my lord?" John said from his knees.

And Jesus said, "John, I can see your house from up here."

The War

An elderly Italian man, well over ninety years old, went to his parish priest and asked if the priest would hear his confession.

"Of course, my son," said the priest.

"Well, Father, at the beginning of World War Two, a Jewish woman knocked on my door and asked me to hide her lovely young daughter from the Germans; I hid her in my attic, and they never found her."

"That's a wonderful thing, my son, and nothing that you need to confess," said the priest.

"It's worse, Father. I was weak, and told the girl that she had to pay for rent of the attic with her sexual favors," continued the old man.

"Well, it was a very difficult time, and you took a large risk - you would have suffered terribly at their hands if the Germans had found you hiding her; I know that God, in his wisdom and mercy, will balance the good and the evil, and judge you kindly," said the priest.

"Thanks, Father," said the old man. "That's a load off of my mind. Can I ask another question?"

"Of course, my son," said the priest.

The old man asked, "Do I need to tell her that the war is over?"

The Dirty Nuns

A man is driving down a deserted stretch of highway in Kentucky when he notices a sign out of the corner of his eye.

It reads: 'SISTERS OF ST. FRANCIS HOUSE OF PROSTITUTION, 10 MILES'

He thinks this is a figment of his imagination and drives on, but soon he sees another sign which reads:

'SISTERS OF ST. FRANCIS HOUSE OF PROSTITUTION, 5 MILES'

Suddenly he begins to realize that these signs are real and drives past a third sign that says:

'SISTERS OF ST. FRANCIS HOUSE OF PROSTITUTION, NEXT RIGHT'

His curiosity gets the best of him and he takes the exit and drives down a dark road which leads to a stone building. The man parks and gets out and finds with a small sign next to the door of the stone building reading:

'SISTERS OF ST. FRANCIS'

He climbs the steps and rings the bell.

The door is answered by a nun in a long black habit who asks, "What may we do for you my son?"

The man almost blushes, but he answers, "I saw your signs along the highway and was interested in possibly doing business..."

"Very well my son. Please follow me."

The man enters and follows the nun. He is led through many winding passages and is soon quite disoriented.

The nun stops at a closed door and tells the man, "Please knock on this door."

He does so and another nun in a long habit, holding a tin cup answers the door.

This nun instructs him, "Please place $500 in the cup then go through the large wooden door at the end of the hallway."

He puts $500 in the cup, eagerly trots down the hall and slips through the door, which shuts behind him.

He finds himself back in the parking lot facing another sign:

'YOU HAVE JUST BEEN SCREWED BY THE SISTERS OF ST. FRANCIS'

The Racehorse

A man was sitting quietly reading the news on his phone when suddenly his wife hit him on the head with a frying pan.

"What was that for?" the man yelped.

The wife replied, "That was for the piece of paper with the name Jenny on it that I found in your pants pocket."

The man rubbed his head and explained, "When I was at the races last week, Jenny was the name of the horse I bet on."

His wife apologized profusely and went back to her housework.

Three days later, the man is watching TV when his wife bashes him on the head with an even bigger frying pan, knocking him unconscious. Upon regaining consciousness, the man asked why she hit again.

Wife replied, "Your horse just called."

Bombing Duke

A young man had a date with a beautiful girl.

Before he went, he made the mistake of eating a jumbo can of beans.

Right after he picked her up, he felt the need to fart, but he figured he could wait until they got to the movies.

When they got there, told her he was going to get them some popcorn and soda, but he used the opportunity to go to the restroom instead.

The line for the restroom was really long, so he went back to the lobby, got the food, and went back into the theater.

When the movie was over, he went to the bathroom again, but there was still a tremendously long line.

So he figured he'd just have to wait until he drops her off.

When they pull up into her driveway, she exclaims, "Oh goodie. My grandparents are here. Come on in and meet them."

He agrees, although he feels he's about to explode. They go in and sit down at the table, making small talk with the girl's grandparents. His face was turning red from the pressure; he really needed to let it out.

Finally, he couldn't hold it in any longer a tried to let it seep out a little at a time. Luckily, the family dog, and old hound dog named Duke, was under the table at his feet.

As he squeezed out a toxic blast, he aimed it towards Duke, in hopes that they might blame the pooch for the horrendous fart.

At the sound, the girl's father stands up and hollers, "Duke!" and sits back down.

"Great!" the young man thought. "They really think it's the dog!"

So he starts bombarding the room with more stinkers, loud and devastatingly pungent.

Once again, the girl's father stands up, shouts "Duke!" and sits back down.

Finally, he lets it all go and the loudest, most hair-curling fart you've ever heard or smelled rippled through the dining room.

The girl's father stands up again and shouts at the dog, "Duke, get the hell out from under him before he shits on you!"

Golfers

A successful married businessman plays a round of golf every day. First thing Monday morning, he sets off on his first round and soon starts to catch up to the player ahead of him on the course. As he gets closer, he notices that the player is a woman; he can tell by the short skirt she's wearing. As he gets even closer to her on the third hole, he notices that she's very attractive.

He watches her bend over as she practices her swing, and he decides, married or not, he has to talk to her. He catches up to her and suggests that they play the rest of the round together. She agrees and a very close match ensues. She turns out to be a very talented golfer and she wins their little competition on the last hole.

He congratulates her in the parking lot, and then offers to give her a lift when he sees she doesn't have a car. All in all, it's been a highly enjoyable morning, and she's been easy on the eyes.

On the way to her place, she thanks him for the morning's company and competition and says she hasn't enjoyed herself so much on the course for a long time.

She looks at him flirtatiously as says, "I'd like you to pull over so I can show you how much I appreciated everything."

He pulls over and the woman kisses him passionately.

The next morning he spies her at the first tee and suggests they play together again. He's actually quite competitive and slightly peeved that she beat him the previous day, but thrilled to be able to watch her again. Again they have a magnificent day, enjoying each other's company and playing a tight, competitive round of golf. Again she beats him on the last hole, and again he drives her home and again she shows her appreciation with a long, hot kiss.

This goes on all week, with her beating him narrowly every day. This is a sore point for his male ego but, nevertheless,

in the car home from their Friday afternoon round, he tells her that he has had such a fine week that he has a surprise planned: dinner for two at a fancy candle-lit restaurant followed by a night of passion in the penthouse apartment of a posh hotel.

Surprisingly, she bursts into tears and says she can't agree to this. He can't work out what the fuss is about but eventually she admits the reason.

"You see," she tearfully sobs, "I'm a transvestite."

The man is aghast. He swerves violently off the road, pulls the car to a screeching halt and curses madly, overcome with emotion.

"I'm sorry," she repeats.

"You bastard," he screams, red in the face, "You dirty lying bastard! You've been playing off the red tees all week!!"

The Cookie

After ten years of marriage, a woman discovers her husband is cheating on her with their attractive young neighbor.

Devastated, she doesn't know how she can continue to live her life. She hears that there's a very wise monk who lives up in a mountain, and decides to go there to consult him.

After days of traveling, hiking, and climbing, she reaches the top of the mountain and meets the wise monk.

"I have spent my whole life with him, my youth was dedicated to support him, to take care of him. And now he has left me for a young woman. My life is stolen, and I'm left with nothing. I don't know what to do," the woman whines.

The monk gives her a cookie and asks her to eat it.

After she finishes eating, he asks, "Was the cookie delicious?"

"Yes," she answers.

"Do you want another one?"

"Sure, please."

The monk looks her in the eye and says "Do you see the problem now?"

The woman thinks for a while, and then slowly speaks.

"I guess human nature is greedy. You get one, then you want more, maybe a new one, bigger one, a younger one. It's never enough. And nothing lasts forever, everything is illusory. We should be aware and not disappointed by that."

The monk shakes his head. "No, I mean you are too fat, you should eat less."

Traveler's Disease

A businessman took a long trip to Asia, stopping in Thailand, China, the Philippines, and Vietnam. While he was there, he cheated on his wife with a different girl in every city. After he returned, he noticed strange growth on his penis. He saw several doctors, but they all give him the same terrifying prognosis.

They all said, "You've been screwing around in the Far East, and this disease is very common there, but there's no cure. We'll have to cut it off."

The man panics, but figures if it is common in the East they must know how to cure it. So he goes back and sees a doctor in Thailand.

The Thai doctor examines his penis closely and says, "You've been fooling around in my country. This is a very common problem here. Did you see any other doctors?"

The man replies, "Yes, I saw several in the USA."

The doctor says, "I bet they told you it had to be cut off."

The man answers, "Yes!"

The Thai doctor smiles, nods, "That's totally wrong."

"Oh, thank God!" the man replied.

The doctor continued, "Yes, it will fall off by itself."

The Jumper

A pretty lady is standing on the side of a bridge, looking over it and thinking about jumping off. A homeless man sees her and walks towards her.

The lady notices the man coming and says: "Go away! There's nothing you can say to me to change my mind, you cannot help me."

"Well, if you're going to kill yourself anyway, why don't we have sex? At least I'll enjoy it," replies the man.

"No way, you're disgusting! Go away!"

The homeless man turns and starts walking away.

The lady yells after him, "Is that all you were going to say to me? Nothing more? Won't you try to convince me that life is worth living that I should not jump off? Where are you going in such a hurry?"

The homeless man shakes his head and says, "I have to make it down to the bottom. If I hurry, you'll still be warm."

The Towel

A man is getting into the shower just as his beautiful young trophy wife is finishing up her shower, when they hear the doorbell ring.

The wife quickly wraps herself in a towel and runs downstairs.

When she opens the door, there stands Bob, the next-door neighbor.

Before she says a word, Bob says, "I'll give you $800 to drop that towel."

After thinking for a moment, the woman drops her towel and stands naked in front of Bob.

After a few seconds, Bob hands her $800 and leaves.

The woman wraps back up in the towel and goes back upstairs.

When she gets to the bathroom, her husband asks, "Who was that?"

"It was Bob from next door," she replies.

"Great," the husband says, "did he say anything about the $800 he owes me?"

The Nursing Home

There was an old man in a nursing home who had felt lonely since his wife had passed, and everyday he would sit at the same bench and stare at the trees in the yard.

And elderly woman walked up to him one day and began to talk to him. She heard his story and was saddened by it, and asked if there was anything she could do to cheer him up.

"Actually," the old man said, "you could hold my penis."

At first the lady thought this was strange, but she figured since she wasn't doing anything bad, just holding his penis. No harm done.

Day after day, she'd meet the guy and hold his penis and they would talk for hours on end. She began to enjoy the time and thought nothing about the penis holding.

One day she went to the spot to find that the man was not there. For the next week she didn't see her friend at the bench and began to worry.

She found a nurse and asked, "Did he pass away?"

The woman held her breath, afraid of the answer.

But the nurse responded, "Oh, no! He's been by the pool everyday for about a week now."

The elderly lady didn't quite understand why, but she walked over to the pool to find him. When she got there, she saw him sitting next to the pool with another woman holding his penis!

"What's this?" she yelled at him. "Was my company not good enough for you? What does this woman have that I don't?"

The man looked up with a smile and said, "Parkinson's."

The Seven Dwarves

The seven dwarves are in Rome and they go on a tour of the city. After a while they go to the Vatican and meet the Pope.

Grumpy, for once, seems to have a lot to say.

He keeps asking the Pontiff questions about the church and, in particular, the nuns.

"Your Holiness, do you have any really short nuns?" Grumpy asks.

"No, my son, all of our nuns are at least five feet tall," smiles the Pope.

"Are you sure? I mean, you wouldn't have any nuns that are, say, about my height? Maybe a little shorter?"

"I'm afraid not. Why do you ask?"

"No reason," replies Grumpy. "But you're positive? Nobody in a habit that's about three feet tall, maybe two-and-a-half feet tall?"

"I'm certain, my vertically-challenged son," says the Pope, trying to hide his curiosity.

"Okay," moans Grumpy.

So the Pope listens to the dwarves as they leave the building.

"What'd he say? What'd he say?" chant the other six dwarves.

Grumpy mutters, "He said they don't have any."

And the other six start chanting, "Grumpy fucked a penguin! Grumpy fucked a penguin!"

The Proud Fathers

Four friends reunited at a party after thirty years. After a few laughs and drinks, one of them had to go to the restroom. The ones who stayed behind began to talk about their kids and their successes.

The first guy says, "I am very proud of my son, he is my pride and joy. He started working at a very successful company at the bottom of the barrel. He studied Economics, Business Administration, and was promoted, began to climb the corporate ladder, becoming the General Manager, and now he is the president of the company. He became so rich that he gave his best friend a top-of-the-line Mercedes Benz for his birthday."

The second guy says, "Damn, that's terrific! My son is also my pride and joy, I am very proud of him. He started working on the ground crew for a very big airline. He went to flight school to become a pilot and managed to become a partner in the company where he now owns the majority of the assets. He became so rich that he gave his best friend a brand new jet for his birthday."

The third guy says, "Well, well, well congratulations! My son is also my pride and joy and he is also very rich. He studied in the best universities and became an engineer. He started his own construction company and became very successful and a multimillionaire. He also has a best friend that he's so generous with: he built an enormous mansion especially for his friend."

The three friends congratulated each other mutually for the successes of their sons.

The fourth friend who earlier had gone to rest room returned and asked, "What's going on, what are all the congratulations for?"

One of the three said, "We were talking about the pride we feel for the successes of our sons. What about your son?"

The fourth man replied, "My son is gay and he makes a living dancing as a stripper at a nightclub."

The three friends said, "Oh wow! What a shame that must be, that is horrible, what a disappointment you must feel."

The fourth man replied, "No, not at all. He is my son and I love him! He is my pride and joy. And he's very lucky too. Did you know that his birthday just passed and the other day he received a beautiful mansion, a brand new jet, and a Mercedes Benz from his three boyfriends?"

The Cave Woman

Why did the cave man drag the cave woman by her hair?

Because if he dragged her by the legs, she'd fill up with dirt.

The Gift

My girlfriend's dog died, so to cheer her up, I got her an identical one.

She was livid, "What am I going to do with two dead dogs?"

Divorce Court

Mickey Mouse and Minnie Mouse were in divorce court and the judge said to Mickey, "You say here that your wife is crazy."

Mickey replied, "No, I didn't. I said she's fucking Goofy."

The Mother-in-Law

I was walking with my wife and we came across her mother being beaten up by six guys.

My wife cried, "Aren't you going to help?"

I said, "Nah, six should be enough."

The Flashlight

A man is walking home from work one day and in a dark alley is approached by a street worker.

She tells him, "Twenty dollars."

He had never been with a street worker before, but it was only twenty dollars. He hands over the money and they start going at it in the alley.

Just then, a couple of police come up with their flashlights and ask, "What are you doing? Are you aware that this is illegal?"

The man, enraged, yells, "This is my wife!"

The police officer replies, "Oh, I'm sorry, sir. I had no idea."

The man replies, "Neither did I until you put the light in her face."

The Widower

A man was so devoted to his sick wife that he decided he would not have sex until she past away. After ten long year of agony, this poor soul passed on. About a month after her death, the man decided it was time to have sex.

He went to a local whorehouse and asked the owner of the house how much it would cost to have sex with one of her young ladies. She told him it would cost $1,000 because she had the best girls in the state.

After his wife's illness, the man had little money. He told the owner about his wife's sickness, his faithfulness to her, and how all of his money was spent to keep her happy and well taken care in her long horrible sickness. He told the owner that he only had $50 and that was all.

The owner thought about it and told him to wait a moment. About five minutes later, the owner came back into the room and told him Sue would be more than willing to help him. The man was shocked – the girl, Sue, was lovely, with smooth skin, lustrous long black hair, long legs, perky breasts, and sparkling eyes.

He went into the room and got naked in bed and inserted his dick into her. It had been over ten years since he had last had sex, and this felt nothing like he remembered. He told her that he did not remember it feeling like this; in fact, it felt like he stuck his dick into a bag of sandpaper.

She told him to give her a minute and she could fix the problem. She went into the bathroom and came back within minutes and said she was ready to satisfy him.

He put his dick back in and it felt so good. He was in ecstasy! He asked the girl what she did to make it feel so much better.

She responded, "Oh, I just picked the scabs and let the puss run."

The Accident

Sheila slipped on the bathroom floor while getting out of the shower. Instead of falling over forwards or backwards, she did the splits and suction-cupped herself to the floor.

She yelled out for her husband, "Bruce! Bruce!"

Bruce came running in.

"Bruce, I've suctioned myself to the floor," she said.

Bruce tried to pull her up to no avail.

"You're stuck fast. I'll go to the neighbors house and ask Wayne to help."

They came back and they both tried to pull her up.

"No way, we can't do it," Wayne said, "so let's try Plan B."

"Plan B," exclaimed Bruce, "what's that?"

"I'll go home and get my hammer and chisel and we'll break the tiles under her," replied Wayne.

"Great idea," Bruce said, "while you're doing that, I'll stay here and play with her nipples."

"Play with her nipples?" Wayne said. "Not exactly a good time for that!"

"No," Bruce replied, "but I reckon if I can get her wet enough, we can slide her into the kitchen where the tiles are cheaper."

The Disease

After seeing some odd symptoms, a guy takes his wife to the doctor.

After examining her, the doctor says, "Your wife either has syphilis or Alzheimer's."

"Well, which one?" the man demands.

"Hard to say," says the doctor.

"Well, what am I supposed to do now?"

"Hmm," says the doctor, "Try this: put her in the car, drive her out into the woods about four or five miles from your home, and drop her off. If she finds her way back, don't fuck her!"

The Plane Crash

A plane was flying over the Pacific Ocean when it crashed on a very small remote island.

The six men on the plane got out and, being gentlemen, they helped the only woman on the plane get out.

After a few days on the island, the men were getting pretty horny. They got together and decided each man would have one night of sex with the woman, and they'd all let her have a rest on the seventh day.

This went on pretty well for first week, but during the second week, things began going down, and by the third week things the situation with the woman was almost impossible.

The men decided to have a meeting to see what could be done about her.

About an hour into the meeting, they decided it was time to bury her.

Outhouse Maintenance

Ma and Pa were two hillbillies living in Western Kentucky out on a farm up in the hills.

Pa discovered that the hole under the outhouse wass full. He goes into the house and tells Ma that he doesn't know what to do to empty the hole.

Ma says, "Why don't you go ask the young'n down the road? He must be smart 'cause he's a college graduate."

So Pa drives down to the neighbor's house and asks him, "Mr. College graduate, my outhouse hole is full, and I don't know what to do to empty it."

The young'n tells him, "Get yourself two sticks of dynamite, one with a short fuse and one with a long fuse. Put them both under the outhouse and light them both at the same time. The first one will go off and shoot the outhouse in the air. While it's in the air the second one will then go off and spread the poop all across your farm, fertilizing your ground. The outhouse should then come back down to the same spot atop the now-empty hole."

Pa thanks the neighbor, then drives to the hardware store and picks up two sticks of dynamite, one with a short fuse and one with a long fuse. He goes home and puts them under the outhouse. He then lights them and runs behind a tree.

All of a sudden, Ma comes running out of the house and into the outhouse!

Off goes the first stick of dynamite, shooting the outhouse into the air.

BOOM! Off goes the second stick of dynamite, spreading poop all over the farm.

WHAM! The outhouse comes crashing back down atop the

hole.

Pa races to the outhouse, throws open the door and asks, "Ma, are you all right??!!"

As she pulls up her panties she says, "Yeah, but I'm sure glad I didn't fart in the kitchen.

The Mexican Grandfather

A Mexican family decided it was time to put their elderly grandfather in a nursing home. All the Hispanic facilities were completely full so they had to put him in an Italian home.

After a few weeks in the Italian facility, they came to visit Grandpa.

"How do you like it here?" asks the grandson.

"It's wonderful! Everyone here is so courteous and respectful," says grandpa.

"We're so happy for you!" gushed his daughter. "We were worried that this was the wrong place for you. You know, since you are a little different from everyone."

"Oh, no! Let me tell you about how wonderfully they treat the residents," the old Mexican said with a big smile. "There's a musician here -- he's 85 years old. He hasn't played the violin in 20 years and everyone still calls him 'Maestro'!"

"There is a judge in here -- he's 95 years old. He hasn't been on the bench in 30 years and everyone still calls him 'Your Honor'!"

"There's a dentist here -- 90 years old. He hasn't fixed a tooth for 25 years and everyone still calls him Doctor!"

"And me -- I haven't had sex for 35 years, and they still call me 'The Fucking Mexican'."

The Gay Baby

Two gay men decide to have a baby. They mix their sperm and have a surrogate mother artificially inseminated. When the baby is born, they rush to the hospital.

Two dozen babies are in the ward, 23 of which are crying and screaming. One, over in the corner, is smiling serenely. A nurse comes by, and to the men's delight, she points out the happy child as theirs.

"Isn't it wonderful?" one of them exclaims. "All these unhappy children, and ours is so happy."

"He's happy now," says the nurse. "But just wait until we take the pacifier out of his ass."

Blondies

A blonde was speeding down the road in her little red sports car and was pulled over by a woman police officer who was also a blonde. The cop asked to see the blonde's driver's license. She dug through her purse and was getting progressively more agitated.

"What does it look like?" she finally asked.

The policewoman replied, "It's square and it has your picture on it."

The driver finally found a pocket mirror, looked at it and handed it to the policewoman.

"Here it is," she said.

The blonde officer looked at the mirror, then handed it back saying, "Okay, you can go. I didn't realize you were a cop."

The Oven

What is the worst thing about being a black Jew?

Having to sit in the back of the oven.

Mexican Biker

Why shouldn't you ever run over a Mexican on a bike?

It's probably your bike.

The Shepherd

What do you call a Muslim with 500 girlfriends?

A shepherd.

The Japanese Girlfriend

What's the worst thing about breaking up with your Japanese girlfriend?

You have to drop the bomb twice before she gets the message.

Sparks Flying

I met a beautiful girl down at the park today.

Sparks flew, she fell at my feet, and we ended up having sex right there and then.

I love my new Taser.

The Virgin

A rich Muslim Sheik was assured he was marrying a sweet young virgin, as his religion requires.

On their wedding night he exposed his dick to her and asked, "Do you know what this is?"

She shook her head no.

He said gently, "It's a penis."

She replied, "Oh no, that's not a penis. Penises are big and black!"

The White Boy

A black boy walks into the kitchen where his mother is baking and accidentally spills the flour on his head.

He turns to his mother and says, "Look Mama, I'm a white boy!"

His mother smacks him, hard, and says, "Go tell your Daddy what you just said!"

The boy finds his father and says, "Look Daddy, I'm a white boy!"

His Daddy bends him over, spanks him, stands the boy back up, and says, "Now, what do you have to say for yourself?"

The boy replies, "I've only been a white boy for five minutes and I already hate you black people!"

Ducks and Skunks

A baby duck and a baby skunk raced across the highway, dodging cars and narrowly escaping death. Their families, however, were all killed by a truck barreling down the highway.

Upon reaching the other side, the little duck tells the baby skunk, "My parents both died and didn't tell me what I am."

"Well," says the baby skunk, "You are yellow and you have a bill and webbed feet. You must be a duck."

The duck thanked him.

The baby skunk then tells the duck, "My parents didn't tell me what I am, either."

"Well," says the baby duck, "You're not quite black and you're not quite white, and you smell bad. You must be Mexican."

The Blondes

A blind black man walks into a lesbian bar. He taps his way to the bar with his cane, sits down, and orders a drink.

When his drink arrives, he asks the bartender, "Wanna hear a blonde joke?"

Bartender says, "Listen, mister, the woman to your left is a three-time world champion weightlifter, and she's a blonde. The woman to your right is a two-time champion mixed martial arts fighter, and she's a blonde. And I've got a 12-gauge shotgun behind the bar, both barrels loaded, and I'm a blonde. Are you sure you want to tell a blonde joke in here?"

The blind black guy thinks about it for a second and says, "Nah, I don't want to have to explain it three times."

The Lesson

A boy says to his dad, "Why do they say gardeners have 'green thumbs' when their thumbs aren't really green?"

The dad replies, "It's just a saying, son. It's like when someone is caught stealing something, they say that they've been caught 'red-handed', even though their hands are actually black."

Modern Art

An eccentric billionaire wanted a mural painted on his library wall so he called a famous artist. Describing what he wanted, the billionaire said, "I am a military history buff and I would like your interpretation of the last thing that went through Custer's mind before he died. I am going out of town on business for a week, and when I return, I expect to see it completed."

Upon his return, the billionaire went to the library to examine the finished work. To his surprise, he found a painting of a cow with a halo in the middle of the wall. Surrounding the cow were hundreds of images of Native Americans in various sexual positions performing all kinds of unspeakable acts. Furious, he called the artist in.

"What the hell is this?" shouted the billionaire.

"Why, that's exactly what you asked for," said the artist smugly.

"No, I didn't ask for a mural of pornographic bestial filth. I asked for an interpretation of Custer's last thoughts!"

"And there you have it," said the artist. "I call it, 'Holy cow, that's a lot of fucking Indians!'"

Actors in Therapy

Three actors are seated in a semicircle. The therapist starts with the 12-year-old boy.

"Johnny, why don't you tell us what happened to you."

Johnny says, "W-w-well... At least three times a year, the theater director, Kevin Spacey, would tell my parents he was taking me to 'acting camp' for a few days which was really a hotel room where he buggered me every night."

Oh Johnny, that's horrible," the therapist said. "We're going help you any way we can."

The therapist then turns to the blonde girl and says, "Jenny why don't you tell us your experience."

"Harvey Weinstein told me that if I didn't suck his dick everyday, he'd had me written out of the show. I was on it for five years," she said before totally breaking down into sobbing wreck.

"Oh Jenny, we are going get you the help you need, even if it take us years."

Then she turns to the other actor and says, "Kermit, why are you here?"

"For 30 years, Jim Henson stuck his hand up my ass and filmed it while I was trying to perform."

The Taxidermist

A black guy walks into a country bar in Alabama and orders a white wine.

Everybody sitting around the bar looks up, surprised, and the bartender looks around and says: "You ain't from around here, are ya? Where ya from, boy?"

The black guy says, "I'm from Iowa."

The bartender asks, "What th' hell you do in Iowa?"

The black guy responds, "I'm a taxidermist. "

The bartender asks, "A taxidermist... now just what th' hell is a taxidermist? "

The black guy says, "I mount animals."

The bartender grins and shouts out to the whole bar, "It's OK, boys, he's one of us!"

The Parrot

A black guy walks into a bar with a parrot on his shoulder and asks for a beer.

The bartender brings a beer and notices the parrot on his shoulder and says, "Hey, that's really neat. Where did you get it?"

The parrot responds, "In the jungle, there's millions of them."

Eileen and Irene

What do you call an Irish girl with one leg shorter than the other?

Eileen.

What do you call a Japanese girl with one leg shorter than the other?

Irene.

Anne Frank

I feel sorry for Anne Frank. First she gets her diary published, which is every girl's worst nightmare, but on top of that she doesn't get any money from it, which is every Jew's worst nightmare.

Burning Eyes

Why do black mens' eyes burn during sex?

Pepper spray.

The Scotsman

A Scotsman was out having a very good time on Saturday night sampling the local whiskey and on the way home, he passed out along the lane.

Later that night, a wind came blowing by and blew his kilt up to his waist as he lie there. Well, we all know what a real Scotsman wears under his kilt.

Early Sunday morning the two little old ladies came by and saw him lying there.

"Prudence have you ever seen such a sight!" one exclaimed.

"No, I haven't Purity. He deserves some kind of punishment."

As she searched her bag, she found something and said, "Here this should do it."

And she tied a ribbon around his member.

"Serves him right," they huffed and continued on to church.

Later the Scotsman awoke and looked down at his member and saw the bright blue ribbon tied around it and said, "Aye Laddie, I dunna know where ye been, but ye won ferst prize!"

The Convert

Two Jews were sitting in front of a church when they noticed a sign tacked on the entrance that said: 'We pay $500 if you convert.' One of them decided to go in.

He came out hours later, and his friend said, "So, did you get the money?"

The other man replied, "Is that all you people think about?"

The Sammy Davis

A black Jewish boy runs home from school one day and asks his father, "Daddy, am I more Jewish or more black?"

The dad replies, "Why do you want to know, son?"

"Because a kid at school is selling a bike for $50 and I want to know if I should talk him down to $40 or just steal it!"

Gay Golf

A gay guy is out taking his first golf lesson. The pro shows him how to place his feet, how to hold the club, and how to swing. Then he puts a ball down and tells the gay guy to hit it.

It goes about 30 feet and hooks.

"Not a bad first try, but let's give it another shot."

The second time, it goes about 25 feet and slices.

"I think I see your problem," says the Pro. "You're not comfortable with the club. Don't hold the club like it's something foreign to you. Pretend it's a penis, and hold it like that."

This time that ball goes sailing 300 yards straight down the fairway and lands about 5 feet from the hole.

"Well, that was very impressive, but why don't you take the club out of your mouth and let's try it again . . ."

The Camels

Why do they call camels "The Ship of the Desert"?

Because they're filled with Arab semen.

The Jewish Father

A Jewish boy asks his father for fifty dollars.

The father replies, "Forty dollars? What do you need thirty dollars for?"

The Gay Life

Two gay guys were sitting at a bar and one says to the other, "I fucked the hottest guy of my life last night."

The other gay guy turns to him and says, "No shit?"

And the other guy replies, "Well, just a little."

The Pickup Truck

There was a redneck who ran over every Mexican he saw with his truck.

One day he saw a black preacher walking down the road and thought, "For all the bad things I done, let me give this preacher a ride."

So he picked the preacher up and they drove along. The redneck saw a Mexican walking down the road and couldn't resist running him over, but he didn't want the preacher to see him do it. He decided he would pretend to fall asleep at the wheel so the preacher would think it was an accident.

The redneck closed his eyes, swerved, and heard a loud thump.

"What happened?" the redneck asked.

"You missed him," the black preacher said, "but I got him with the door."

The Trans-Rancher

A successful rancher died and left everything to his devoted wife. She was determined to keep the ranch, but knew very little about ranching, so she placed an ad in the newspaper for a ranch hand. Two cowboys applied for the job. One was gay and the other a drunk.

She thought long and hard about it, and when no one else applied she decided to hire the gay guy, figuring it would be safer to have him around the house than the drunk.

He proved to be a hard worker who put in long hours every day and knew a lot about ranching. For weeks, the two of them worked hard and the ranch was doing very well.

Then one day, the rancher's widow said, "You've done a really good job, and the ranch looks great. You should go into town and kick up your heels."

The hired hand readily agreed and went into town on Saturday night. He returned around 2:30 am, and upon entering the ranch main room, he found the rancher's widow sitting by the fireplace with a glass of wine, waiting for him.

She quietly called him over to her. "Unbutton my blouse and take it off," she said.

Trembling, he did as she directed.

"Now take off my boots."

He did as she asked, ever so slowly.

"Now take off my socks."

He removed each gently and placed them neatly by her boots.

"Now take off my skirt."

He slowly unbuttoned it, constantly watching her eyes in the firelight.

"Now take off my bra."

Again, with trembling hands, he did as he was told and dropped it to the floor.

Then she looked at him and said: "If you ever wear my clothes into town again, you're fired."

The First Grade

After Tyrone's first day in the first grade, he came home crying.

When his mother asked why, he replied, "The teacher told us to say our ABC's and all the little white boys could say them and I could only get to the letter E. Why is that?"

His mom said, "Because you black and they white."

The next day Tyrone was crying again.

"What's wrong today, Tyrone?" his mother asked.

Tyrone said, "Teacher told us to count to 100 and all the little white boys did but I could only get up to 10. Why is that?"

The mom answered, "Because you black and they white."

The third day he came home smiling. "What happened today, Tyrone?" asked his mom.

"We went to the bathroom and my thing was biggest of all, because I'm black and they white, right mama?"

She said, "No, Tyrone, it's because you 17 and they 6."

The Immigrant

One of Trump's ICE agents catches an illegal alien in the bushes right by the border fence, he pulls him out by the hair and says, "Sorry, you know the law, you've got to go back across the border right now."

The Mexican man pleads with them, "No, noooo Senor, I must stay in de USA! Pleeeze!"

The ICE agent feels sorry for him, thinking that soon Trump's wall will go up and they'll all be trapped in Mexico. So he decides to give him a chance.

The agent says, "Ok, I'll let you stay if you can use three English words in a sentence. The three words are 'green,' 'pink,' and 'yellow'."

The Mexican man thinks hard, then says, "Hmmm, okay. The phone, it went green, green, green. I pink it up and sez yellow?"

The Teacher

After picking her son up from school one day, the mother asks him what he did at school.

The kid replied, "I had sex with my teacher."

She gets so mad that when they get home, she orders him to go straight to his room. When the father returns home that evening, the mother angrily tells him what their son had done and demands that he contact the police, the school principal, and a lawyer.

But as the father hears the news, a huge grin spreads across his face. The father walks to his son's room and asks him what happened at school.

The boy tells him, "I had sex with my teacher."

The father tells the boy that he is so proud of him, and he is going to reward him with the bike he's wanted for months. As they're leaving the store, the dad asks his son if he would like to ride his new bike home.

His son responds, "No thanks, Dad, my butt still hurts from having sex with my teacher."

Christmas Presents

Tommy asked his friend, "So what did you get for Christmas?"

His friend replied, "I got a bike, a go-kart, an Xbox with 30 games, a PlayStation with 30 games, an electric guitar, a drum kit, a new iPad, a new watch, loads of clothes, loads of candy, a trip to Disneyland, and more!"

To which Tommy replied, "Aww, I wish I had Leukemia."

Catholic School

Little Johnny was going to a public school and he was doing very badly in math, so his mother decided to put him into a Catholic school.

When she got his report card at the end of the term, his grade in math had improved tremendously: little Johnny had earned an A! His mother was shocked and delighted.

So she asked him, "Johnny, how did your math grade improve so quickly?"

He replied, "When I saw that naked guy nailed to the plus sign, I knew they meant business!"

The Baby

A woman visits the doctor because she's been suffering from some abdominal pains and suspects she may be pregnant.

After he finishes examining her, the doctor comes out to see her and says, "Well, I hope you like changing diapers."

The woman replies excitedly, "Oh my God! Am I pregnant, am I pregnant!?"

The doctor says, "No, you've got rectal cancer."

English Lesson

In school, Sarah's teacher says, "Today we are going to learn about multisyllabic words, class. Does anybody have an example of a multisyllabic word?"

Sarah waves her hand, "Me, Miss Rogers, me, me!"

Miss Rogers says, "All right, Sarah, what is your multisyllabic word?"

Sarah says, "Mas-tur-bate."

Miss Rogers blushes, shocked, and says, "Wow, Sarah, that's a mouthful."

Sarah says, "No, Miss Rogers, you're thinking of a blowjob."

Battle of the Sexes

One day, a little boy and a little girl were fighting about the differences between the sexes, and which one is better.

After much arguing to and fro, the boy drops his pants and says, "Here's something I have that you'll never have."

The little girl was upset because what the boy said is obviously true. So she runs home to her Mom, crying. A short time later, she comes running back with a smile on her face.

She sticks her tongue out at the boy, drops her pants, and says, "My Mommy says that with one of these, I can have as many of those as I want!"

The Difference

A young boy walks into the bathroom whilst his father is in the shower and asks, "What's that big hairy thing between your legs, dad?"

"That's a penis, son," replies his father.

"When will I get one of those?" asks the boy, looking down at his own small hairless penis.

"Oh, when you're all big and grown up," says dad.

A short while later his young daughter walks into the bathroom and asks, "What's that between your legs, dad?"

"That's a penis, sweetheart," replies her dad.

"When will I get one of those?" the girl asks.

"Oh, in about 30 minutes, when your mother goes out," replies her dad.

Disciplining Children

One day, Steve's mom was cleaning his room. In the closet, she found a dirty magazine full of the raunchiest photos of men in bondage gear doing unspeakable things to each other. She was horrified as she turned the pages. She wasn't sure how to handle the situation, so she hid the magazine until the boy's father got home.

When Steve's father walked in the door, she irately handed the magazine to him, and said, "This is what I found in your son's closet!"

He looked at it and handed it back to her without a word.

After an uncomfortable minute of silence she finally demanded, "Well, what should we do about this?"

The boy's father looked at her and said, "Well, I don't think you should spank him."

The Van

A man in a van stops little Johnny walking down street and says, "Hey little boy, I'll give you a piece of candy if you come in my van."

Little Johnny says, "How about you give me the whole bag and I'll come on your face!"

The Volunteers

Two guys in a car get pulled over by a cop. The cop walks over and taps the window. The driver rolls it down.

The cop says, "Good evening gentlemen, we're looking for two pedophiles."

The driver quickly closes the window, and the cop sees the two men inside having an animated conversation.

A few seconds later, the driver lowers the window again and says, "Okay, we'll do it."

The Argument

Two pedophiles were walking down the street when they came across a pair of tiny white lace panties on the ground.

The first one picks them up, smells them and says, "Ahhh... A seven-year-old girl."

The other grabs them from him and also takes a smell and says, "No, no... Definitely an eight-year-old girl!"

The two of them take turns smelling them, and then arguing.

"An eight-year-old!"

"No, a seven-year-old!"

"Definitely an eight-year-old!"

The local priest is walking past as the two men argue and can't help but ask them what the commotion is all about. The first pedophile tells the priest, and asks him if he could sort out the argument.

The priest takes the panties, has a good long sniff, and after pondering for a few moments he looks at the two men and says, "Definitely an eight-year-old girl. But not from my church!"

The Date

A guy goes to pick up his date for the evening. She's not ready yet, so he has to sit in the living room with her parents.

The poor guy has a bad case of gas and really needs to relieve some pressure. Luckily, the family dog jumps up on the couch next to him. He decides that he can let a little fart out, and if anyone notices they will think that the dog did it.

He farts, and the woman yells, "Spot, get down from there."

The guy thinks, "Great, they think the dog did it."

He releases another fart, and the woman again yells for the dog to get down. This goes on for a couple more farts.

Finally the woman yells, "Dammit, Spot, get down before he shits on you."

The Hospital Visit

John is paying a visit to his Italian neighbor in the hospital, who just had a very serious traffic accident. He doesn't look like very much: in plaster, completely wrapped in a bandage, tons of tubes in his veins. He looks like a mummy. John tries to have a conversation, but his neighbor has his eyes closed and isn't responding.

Suddenly, his eyes jump wide open, and he starts to gurgle ,and during his last gasp for air, he says: "Mi stai bloccando il d'tubicino ossigeno, Pezzo di merda..."

John inscribes the words in his heart. At the funeral John tells the black-clad widow that her husband had something to say.

"What was it?" she asks with tearful eyes, "Was it that he loved me?"

"I don't know," said the man, "but it sounded like 'Mi stai bloccando il d'tubicino ossigeno, pezzo di merda'."

The widow screams and faints.

John turns, startled, to the daughter and asks, "What did he say? What does that mean?"

And the crying daughter says: "It means, 'You're standing on my oxygen hose, you ass'."

The English Prince

Police arrested Prince Harry, the son of Prince Charles, second in line to the throne, late one night. Prince Harry was charged with lewd and lascivious behavior, public indecency, drunk driving, and public intoxication at the County courthouse on Monday. Of course, the entire country was shocked by the allegations and followed the case closely.

The police officer testified before the judge that he witnessed Prince Harry leaving a pub after a night drinking with his lads. Prince Harry got into his car and drove towards Windsor Castle. Because the car was weaving, the office suspected Prince Harry of drunk driving.

Then the officer testified that Prince Harry pulled the car over next to a roadside pumpkin patch.

"I suspected the defendant would attempt to urinate in public after drinking so much," the officer testified, "so I followed him into the pumpkin patch."

What the officer witnessed next shocked the English public long inured to royal scandal.

"When I got up close to him in the dark, I witnessed the Prince fornicating with a pumpkin!"

A gasp arose in the courtroom.

The judge looked down at the officer from his bench and asked, "Did you then confront the Defendant?"

The officer nodded, "I just went up and said, 'Excuse me, your highness, but do you realize that you are screwing a pumpkin?'"

There were titters of laughter in the courtroom.

"Silence!" the judge ordered, banging his gavel. "How did the Defendant respond?"

"Well, Prince Harry, he got real surprised to see me there in the dark, as you'd expect, and then looked me straight in the face and said, 'A pumpkin? Damn. Is it midnight already?'"

The Hunter

A hunter goes into the woods to hunt a bear. He carries his trusty 22-gauge rifle with him. After a while, he spots a very large bear, takes aim, and fires. When the smoke clears, the bear is gone.

A moment later, the bear taps the hunter on the shoulder and says, "No one shoots at me and gets away with it. You have two choices: I can rip your throat out and eat you, or you can drop your trousers, bend over, and I'll screw you."

The hunter decides that anything is better than death, so he drops his trousers and bends over, and the bear does what he said he would do. After the bear has left, the hunter pulls up his trousers and staggers back into town.

He's pretty mad. He buys a much larger gun and returns to the forest. He sees the same bear, aims, and fires. When the smoke clears, the bear is gone.

A moment later the bear taps the hunter on the shoulder and says, "You know what to do."

Afterward, the hunter pulls up his trousers, crawls back into town, and buys a bazooka. Now he's really mad. He returns to the forest, sees the bear, aims, and fires. The force of the bazooka blast knocks him flat on his back.

When the smoke clears, the bear is standing over him and says, "You're not doing this for the hunting, are you?"

The Puppy

While on an out-of-town trip, a man got a small puppy as a present for his son. Not having time to get the paperwork to take the puppy on board, the man just hid the pup down the front of his pants and snuck him on board the airplane. About 30 minutes into the trip, a stewardess noticed the man shaking and quivering.

"Are you okay, sir?" asked the stewardess.

"Yes, I'm fine," said the man.

Later, the stewardess noticed the man moaning and shaking again.

"Are you sure you're alright sir?"

"Yes," said the man, "but I have a confession to make. I didn't have time to get the paperwork to bring a puppy on board, so I hid him down the front of my pants."

"What's wrong?" asked the stewardess. "Is he not house trained?"

"No, that's not the problem. The problem is he's not weaned yet!"

The Rooster

A farmer's chickens aren't laying as many eggs anymore, so he goes out and buys a new, young rooster. As soon as he brings him home, the young rooster rushes into the chicken coop and screws all hundred of the farmer's hens.

The farmer is impressed.

At lunchtime, the young rooster again screws all hundred hens. The farmer is impressed, but a little worried. The next morning, not only is the rooster screwing the hens, but he is also screwing the turkeys, ducks, and even the cow. Now the farmer is seriously concerned. Later that afternoon, the farmer looks out into the barnyard and sees the rooster stretched out on the ground, his wings flung wide, his eyes closed, and vultures circling overhead.

The farmer runs out, looks down at the young rooster's limp body, and says: "You deserved it, you horny bastard!"

And the young rooster opens one eye, points up at the vultures with his wing, and says, "Shhhh! They're about to land."

The Fishing Trip

Five friends were playing poker and planning their upcoming fishing trip.

One of them, Steve, he had to tell them that he couldn't go because his wife wouldn't let him. After a lot of teasing and name-calling, Steve headed home, frustrated. The following week when Steve's buddies arrived at the lake to set up camp, they were shocked to see Steve. He was already sitting at the campground with a cold beer, fishing rod in hand, and a campfire glowing.

"How did you talk your missus into letting you go, Steve?"

"I didn't have to," Steve replied. "Yesterday, when I left work, I went home and slumped down in my chair with a beer to drown my sorrows because I couldn't go fishing. Then my wife snuck up behind me and covered my eyes and said, 'Surprise!'"

"When I pulled her hands back, she was standing there in red lingerie. She said to me, 'Carry me into the bedroom, tie me to the bed, and do whatever you want,' so I tied her to the bed and went fishing."

The Rodeo

Two cowboys are having a beer at a bar and talking about sex.

The first cowboy says, "I like the rodeo position."

"Can't say I've heard of the rodeo position," the second cowboy says as he takes a drink of beer. "What is it?"

"Well, you get a girl down on all fours and mount her from behind. Then you reach round and cup both of her breasts and whisper in her ear, 'These feel just like your sister's tits.' Then you try to hold on for 8 seconds!"

The Family Man

A man walked into a bar and says to the bartender, "Gimme five shots of whiskey."

The bartender asks, "What's the matter?"

The man says, "I found out my brother is gay and marrying my best friend."

The next day, the same man comes in and orders ten shots of whiskey.

The bartender asks, "What's wrong this time?"

The man says, "I found out my son is gay."

The next day the same man comes in the bar and orders fifteen shots of whiskey.

The bartender asks, "Doesn't anyone in your family like women?"

The man looks up and says, "Apparently my wife does."

The Salesman

A young guy from Nebraska moves to Florida and goes to a big box store looking for a job.

The manager says, "Do you have any sales experience?"

The kid says, "Yeah. I was a salesman back in Omaha."

The manager liked the kid and gave him the job.

"You start tomorrow. I'll come down after we close and see how you did."

His first day on the job was rough, but he got through it. After the store was locked up, the manager came down.

"How many customers bought something from you today?"

The kid says, "One."

The boss says, "Just one? Our sales people average 20 to 30 customers a day. How much was the sale for?"

The kid says, "$101,237.65."

The boss says, in shock, "$101,237.65? What the heck did you sell?"

The kid says, "First, I sold him a small fish hook. Then I sold him a medium fishhook. Then I sold him a large fishhook. Then I sold him a new fishing rod. Then I asked him where he was going fishing and he said down the coast, so I told him he was going to need a boat, so we went down to the boat department and I sold him a twin engine Boston Whaler. Then he said he didn't think his Honda Civic would pull it, so I took him down to the automotive department and sold him that 4x4 Expedition."

The boss said, incredulous, "A guy came in here to buy a fish hook and you sold him a BOAT and a TRUCK?"

The kid said, "No, the guy came in here to buy tampons for his wife, and I said, 'Dude, your weekend's shot, you should go fishing.'"

Kermit

One day, Kermit the Frog was looking sad. Fozzie Bear went up to him and asked what was wrong.

Kermit said, "I'm having problems with Miss Piggy."

"Like what?" asked Fozzie.

"Well, Miss Piggy wants me to eat her out and I can't."

Fozzie asked, "So, what's wrong with that? What are you, a prude?"

"No," sighed Kermit, "but I am a Jew."

The Fence

Two rednecks, Bubba and Billy Bob, were walking through a pasture. Bubba sees a sheep caught up in a fence and says to Billy Bob, "I'm gonna get me some of that!"

Bubba walks over the sheep, stuck to the fence, and unzips his pants and starts to have sex with the sheep.

He looks over his shoulder at Billy Bob and says, "Do you want some of this?"

Billy Bob replies, "Yeah, let me see if I can get my shirt caught up in the fence".

The Beach

A man is lying on the beach sunbathing, wearing nothing but a cap over his dick.

A woman passes by and remarks, "If you were a gentleman, you would lift your hat for a lady."

The man replies, "If you were any sort of lady, the hat would lift itself!"

The Itch

A guy picks up a prostitute and spends a couple hours with her at a seedy motel. A few days later, he finds that he has a nasty case of crabs.

He chases down the prostitute and says, "Hey, bitch, you gave me crabs!"

She replies, "What'd you expect for twenty bucks? Lobster?"

The Barbershop

A man brought his daughter with him to the barbershop on a Saturday afternoon. The cute little girl stood right next to the chair where her father was getting his haircut. The barber looked down at her and saw she was eating a Twinkie.

"Sweetheart," the barber said to the girl, "You're going to get hair on your Twinkie."

"I know," nodded the little girl. "And I'm going to get boobies, too."

The Whorehouse

A guy walks in the local whorehouse and says "I want the cheapest one you got; I don't have much money."

The guy behind the counter says, "How bout the $1.95 cent special?"

The customer says, "Great!"

He pays and happily heads to the room. When he opens the door, he finds a remarkably beautiful young girl lying on the bed, naked with her legs wide open, just waiting for him. He rips off his clothes and starts going to town on her.
Suddenly, all this white stuff starts coming out of her mouth, nose, and even her ears.

The man panics and jumps out of bed. He runs to the desk and tells the guy what happened.

The guy just nods and then says to the janitor, "Hey, Joe? The dead one's full again."

The Prostitute

Harry and his wife are having hard financial times, so they decide that she'll become a hooker.

She's not quite sure what to do, so Harry says, "Stand in front of that bar and pick up a guy. Tell him that you charge a hundred bucks. If you got a question, I'll be parked around the corner."

She's standing there for vie minutes when a guy pulls up and asks, "How much?"

She says, "A hundred dollars."

He says, "All I got is thirty".

"Hold on," she says, and runs back to Harry and asks, "What can he get for thirty dollars?"

"A hand job," Harry replies.

She runs back and tells the guy all he gets for thirty dollars is a hand job. He agrees, and she gets in his car. He unzips his pants and out pops an enormous penis.

She stares at it for a minute, and then says, "I'll be right back."

She runs back to Harry, and asks, "Can you loan this guy seventy bucks?"

The Nuns

A bus full of nuns drives off a cliff, and sadly they all die in a fiery crash. They arrive at the gates of heaven and meet St. Peter.

St. Peter says to them "Sisters, welcome to Heaven. In a moment I will let you all though the pearly gates, but first I must ask each of you a single question. Please form a single-file line."

And they do so. St. Peter turns to the first nun in the line and asks her "Sister, have you ever touched a penis?"

The nn responds, "Well... there was this one time... that I kinda sorta... touched one with the tip of my pinky finger..."

St. Peter says "Alright, Sister, now dip the tip of your pinky finger in the Holy Water, and you may be admitted," and she did so.

St. Peter now turns to the second nun and says "Sister, have you ever touched a penis?"

"Well... There was this one time... that I held one for a moment..."

"Alright Sister, now just wash your hands in the Holy Water, and you may be admitted," and she does so.

At this, there is a jostling in the back of the line as one nun is trying to cut in front of another.

St. Peter sees this and asks the nun, "Sister Susan, what's the matter? There's no rush!"

Sister Susan responds, "Well, if I'm going to have to gargle the stuff, I'd rather do it before Sister Mary sticks her ass in it!"

The Train

A few days after Christmas, a mother was working in the kitchen listening to her young son playing with his new electric train in the living room.

She heard the train stop and her son said, "All of you sons of bitches who want off, get the hell off now, 'cause this is the last stop! And all of you sons of bitches who are getting on, get your asses in the train, cause we're going down the tracks."

The mother went nuts and told her son, "We don't use that kind of language in this house. Now I want you to go to your room and you are to stay there for TWO HOURS. When you come out, you may play with your train, but I want you to use nice language."

Two hours later, the son comes out of the bedroom and resumes playing with his train.

Soon the train stopped and the mother heard her son say, "All passengers who are disembarking from the train, please remember to take all of your belongings with you. We thank you for riding with us today and hope your trip was a pleasant one. We hope you will ride with us again soon."

She hears the little boy continue, "For those of you just boarding, we ask you to stow all of your hand luggage under your seat. Remember, there is no smoking on the train. We hope you will have a pleasant and relaxing journey with us today."

As the mother began to smile, the child added, "For those of you who are pissed off about the TWO HOUR delay, please see the bitch in the kitchen."

Prison Break

A man escapes from prison where he has been for 15 years. He breaks into a house to look for money and guns and finds a young couple in bed. He orders the guy out of bed and ties him to a chair, while tying the girl to the bed he gets on top of her, kisses her neck, then gets up and goes into the bathroom.

While he's in there, the husband tells his wife: "Listen, this guy's an escaped convict, look at his clothes! He probably spent lots of time in jail and hasn't seen a woman in years. I saw how he kissed your neck. If he wants sex, don't resist, don't complain, do whatever he tells you. Satisfy him no matter how much he nauseates you. This guy is probably very dangerous. If he gets angry, he'll kill us. Be strong, honey. I love you."

To which his wife responds: "He wasn't kissing my neck. He was whispering in my ear. He told me he was gay, thought you were cute, and asked me if we had any vaseline. I told him it was in the bathroom. Be strong honey. I love you too!"

The Shrink

A psychiatrist was conducting a group therapy session with three young mothers and their small children.

"You all have obsessions," he observed.

To the first mother, he said, "You are obsessed with eating. You've even named your daughter Candy."

He turned to the second mom. "Your obsession is money. Again, it manifests itself in your child's name, Penny."

At this point, the third mother got up, took her little boy by the hand and whispered, "Come on, Dick, let's go."

The Proposal

Jim decided to propose to Sandy, but before she could accept, Sandy confessed to Jim that she'd suffered a childhood illness that left her breasts at the maturity of a twelve-year-old.

Jim told her he loved her so much that it didn't matter to him at all, her loved her just the way she was.

But Jim had a confession of his own: "I, too, have a problem. My penis is the same size as an infant and I hope you can deal with that once we are married."

Sandy was a little disappointed, but she loved Jim, and he was so willing to overlook her flaw that she decided she would overlook his.

Sandy said, "Yes, Jim, I will marry you and learn to live with your infant-sized penis."

Sandy and Jim got married, and as soon as they arrived in their hotel suite, they couldn't keep their hands off each other. As Sandy put her hand in Jim's pants, she suddenly screamed and ran out of the room.

Jim ran after her to find out what was wrong.

She said, "You told me your penis was the size of an infant!"

"Yes, it is," Jim insisted, "It's eight pounds, seven ounces, and nineteen inches long!"

The Examination

A beautiful woman one day walks into a doctor's office and the doctor is bowled over by how stunningly awesome she is. All his professionalism goes right out the window. He tells her to take her pants, she does, and he starts rubbing her thighs.

"Do you know what I am doing?" asks the doctor.

"Yes, checking for abnormalities," she replies.

He tells her to take off her shirt and bra, she takes them off.

The doctor begins rubbing her breasts and asks, "Do you know what I am doing now?"

She replies, "Yes, checking for cancer."

Finally, he tells her to take off her panties, lays her on the table, climbs on top of her, and starts having sex with her.

He says to her, "Do you know what I am doing now?"

She replies, "Yes, getting herpes – that's why I'm here!"

The Operation

A patient was in the intensive care unit recovering from surgery. He was wearing an oxygen mask over his mouth and nose and lying on hospital bed. A young nurse came to clean his body with a sponge.

The patient mumbled, "Are my testicles black?"

The nurse replied, "I don't know, sir, I'm just here for your bath."

The patient repeated again from behind his mask, "Are my testicles black?"

Nurse was embarrassed by the question and said, "Sir, you'll need to talk to your doctor about that."

The patient just kept on asking again and again, "Are my testicles black?"

The nurse couldn't bear it any longer: the patient was clearly in misery. So she raised his gown, leaned her head over closely, took his penis in her hand, and carefully checked his testicles.

Suddenly, the man ejaculated on the nurse's hand.

The man pulled off his oxygen mask and said, "Thanks for that, but I still need to know: 'Are my tests results back?'"

The Squirrels

This young boy named Don walked into a whorehouse, slammed his money on the counter and said, "I want a woman!"

The man behind the counter asked, "How old are you?"

Don replied, "I'm 17!"

The man said, "You're too young, come back when you're older; meanwhile, practice on trees."

"Trees?" Don asked.

"Yeah," the man nodded, "Go find yourself a nice hole in a tree."

A year later Don once again came back to the whorehouse, swung the front door open, stomped over to the front desk and slammed his money on the counter harder than before.

He screamed, "GIVE ME A WOMAN!"

The man behind the counter said, "How old are you?"

Don grinned, "I'm 18!"

The man took Don's money and said, "OK, upstairs, second door on the left."

Don didn't miss a beat. He ran up those stairs so fast he skipped every other step. About five minutes later, the man behind the counter heard the whore upstairs screaming in complete and utter agony. He jumped over the counter and ran up the stairs. Once at the room he kicked in the door and, to his surprise, Don had a broomstick shoved right into the poor girl.

The man shouted, "WHAT ARE YOU DOING?"

Don simply replied, "Checking for squirrels..."

The Birds and the Bees

One night a little girl walks in on her parents having sex. The mother is going up and down on the father, and when she sees her daughter looking at them, she immediately stops.

The little girl ask, "What are you doing, Mommy?"

The mother, too embarrassed to tell her little girl about sex, makes up an answer.

"Well, sweetie, sometimes daddy's tummy gets too big so I have to jump up and down on it to flatten it out."

The little girl replies, "Well, mommy you really shouldn't bother with that."

The mother has a confused look on her face, "Why do you say that, sweetheart?"

The little girl replies, "Because mommy, every time you leave in the morning, the lady next door comes over and blows it back up."

The Reporter

When a man in Macon, Georgia came upon a wild dog attacking a young boy, he quickly grabbed the animal and throttled it with his two hands.

A reporter heard about the incident and called to congratulate the man. He told him the headline the following day would read, "Local Man Saves Child by Killing Vicious Animal."

The hero, however, told the journalist that he wasn't from Macon.

"Well, then," the reporter said with some disdain, "the headline will probably say, "Georgia Man Saves Child by Killing Dog."

"Actually," the man said, "I'm from Connecticut."

"In that case," the reporter said in a huff, "the headline will read, "Yankee Kills Family Pet."

Hypothetically Speaking

A little boy came home from school and struggled with his homework assignment. He needed to explain the difference was between 'hypothetically' and 'realistically', so he asked his dad.

His dad said, "Well, go ask your mom if she would sleep with the mailman for one million dollars."

The boy went and asked, and came back and said, "Mom said yes."

"Well," said the dad, "Go ask your sister if she'd sleep with the mailman for one million dollars."

The boy did, and came back and said, "She said yes."

And the dad said, "Now go ask your brother the same thing."

He did and came back and said, "He said yes too!"

The dad explained, "Well, hypothetically, we're sitting on three million dollars, but realistically we're living with two whores and a gay kid!"

The Cat

Little Johnny comes down to breakfast. Since they live on a farm, his mother asks if he had done his chores.

"Not yet," said Little Johnny.

His mother tells him no breakfast until he does his chores. Well, he's a little pissed off, so he goes to feed the chickens, and he kicks a chicken. He goes to feed the cows, and he kicks a cow. He goes to feed the pigs and he kicks a pig. He goes back in for breakfast and his mother gives him a bowl of dry cereal.

"Why don't I get any eggs and bacon? Why don't I have any milk in my cereal?" he asks.

"Well," his mother says, "I saw you kick a chicken, so you don't get any eggs for a week. I saw you kick the pig, so you don't get any bacon for a week either. I also saw you kick the cow, so for a week you aren't getting any milk."

Just then, his father comes down for breakfast and kicks the cat halfway across the kitchen.

Little Johnny looks up at his mother with a smile, and says: "Are you going to tell him, or should I?"

Rigor Mortis

Little Billy came home from school to see the family's pet rooster dead in the front yard. Rigor mortis had set in and the bird was flat on its back with its legs in the air.

When his Dad came home, Billy said, "Dad, our rooster's dead and his legs are sticking in the air. Why are his legs sticking in the air?"

His father thinking quickly said, "Son, that's so God can reach down from the clouds and lift the rooster straight up to heaven."

"Gee Dad that's great," said little Billy.

A few days later, when Dad came home from work, Billy rushed out to meet him yelling, "Dad, Dad we almost lost Mom today!"

"What do you mean?" his father asked.

"Well Dad, I got home from school early today and went up to your bedroom and there was Mom flat on her back with her legs in the air, screaming, "Jesus, I'm coming, I'm coming!"

"If it hadn't of been for Uncle George holding her down we'd have lost her for sure!"

The Cookie

One night Little Timmy sees his Dad drinking bourbon.

Little Timmy asks his dad, "Can I have some?"

His dad asks, "Can your dick touch your ass?"

Timmy replies, "No."

"Then no," his Dad replies.

Later on he catches his dad looking at porn.

Timmy asks, "Can I look with you, Daddy?"

His dad asks again "Can your dick touch your ass?"

"No," Timmy answers.

"Then no."

Later that night, Little Timmy is eating cookies.

His dad walks into the kitchen and asks, "Can I have a cookie?"

Timmy asks, "Can your dick touch your ass?"

His dad grins and replies, "Yes."

"Then go fuck yourself -- these cookies are mine!"

The Accident

A young man was showing off his new sports car to his girlfriend. She was thrilled at the speed and raw power and throaty exhaust.

"If I do 200 mph, will you take off your clothes?" he asked.

"Yes!" said his adventurous girlfriend.

And as he gets up to 200, she peeled off all her clothes. Unable to keep his eyes on the road, the car skidded onto some gravel and flipped over. The naked girl was thrown clear, but he was jammed beneath the steering wheel.

"Go and get help!" he cried.

"But I can't! I'm naked and my clothes are gone!" she exclaimed.

"Take my shoe", he said, "and cover yourself."

Holding the shoe in front of her, the girl ran down the road and found a service station. Still holding the shoe between her legs, she pleaded to the service station proprietor, "Please help me! My boyfriend's stuck!"

The proprietor looked at the shoe and said, "There's nothing I can do. He's in too far."

The Burger

A guy walks into a diner and sees a sign hanging over the bar that reads:

CHEESEBURGER: $9.50

CHICKEN SANDWICH: $10.50

HAND JOB: $50.00

He walks up to the bar and beckons to one of the three exceptionally attractive blondes serving drinks.

"Can I help you?" she asks.

"I was wondering," whispers the man. "Are you the one who gives the hand jobs?"

"Yes," she purrs. "I am."

The man replies, "Well, wash your hands. I want a cheeseburger."

The Paint Job

Mother Superior tells two new nuns that they have to paint their room without getting any paint on their clothes.

So the one nun says to the other, "Hey, let's take all our clothes off, fold them up, and lock the door."

So they do this, and begin painting their room naked. Soon they hear a knock at the door.

They ask, "Who is it?"

A man's voice responds, "Blind man!"

The nuns look at each other, then one nun says, "He's blind, he can't see. What could it hurt?"

They open the door and let him in.

The blind man walks in and says, "Hey, nice tits. Where do you want me to hang the blinds?"

Marriage

Two men sitting in a bar commiserating about their lives. One says, "After ten years of marriage, sex is down to three times a year."

The other man replies, "Same here, pal, and as a matter of fact, if my wife didn't sleep with her mouth open I'd have none at all."

Bar Talk

A man in a bar turns to the woman next to him and says, "Hey, I heard an interesting stat the other day. They said that 80% of women masturbate in the shower. Know what the other 20% do?"

"No, what?"

"Yeah, I figured you were in the first group."

Dear Santa

One day, a little boy wrote to Santa Claus, "Please send me a little baby sister."

Santa Clause wrote him back, "OK, send me your mother."

The Secretary

A manager had just hired a new secretary. She was young, sweet, and polite. One day while taking dictation, she noticed his fly was open.

While leaving his office, she courteously said, "Oh, sir, did you know that your barracks door is open?"

He did not understand her remark, but later on, he happened to look down and saw that his zipper was open. He decided to have some fun with his new employee.

Calling her in, he asked, "By the way, Miss Jones, when you saw my barracks door open this morning, did you also see a soldier standing at attention?"

The secretary, who was quite witty, replied, "Why, no, sir. All I saw was a little, disabled veteran, sitting on two duffel bags!"

Girls Night Out

Walking home after a girls' night out, two drunk women pass a graveyard and stop to pee. The first woman has nothing to wipe with, so she uses her underwear and tosses it.

Her friend, however, finds a ribbon on a wreath, so she uses that.

The next day, the first woman's husband phones the second woman's husband, furious: "My wife came home last night without her panties!"

"That's nothing," says the other. "Mine came back with a card stuck between her butt cheeks that said, 'From all of us at the fire station, we'll never forget you.'"

Weight Loss

Over the years, a former athlete had gained a lot of weight. He decided to go to a weight loss clinic where he says he needs to lose twenty pounds. The receptionist sends him upstairs, where he finds a beautiful naked woman with a sign that says, "If you catch me, you can screw me."

For a full day, he chases the girl around and eventually he catches her. He emerges, sated, and twenty pounds lighter.

A month later, he returns, determined to lose fifty pounds. The receptionist sends him upstairs again, but this time there are two girls with the same sign.

Two days later, he comes out fifty pounds lighter.

A year later, he returns, but this time he says he needs to lose a hundred pounds.

He gets sent upstairs again, but this time he finds a huge gorilla with a sign that reads, "If I catch you, I screw you."

The Lawnboy

A man was shaving in the bathroom when all of a sudden Ethan, the boy he pays to mow his lawn, comes in to take a piss. Well, the man can't help but look over his shoulder and he is surprised at the size of the young man's penis.

"Ethan, what's your secret?" the man asks.

Ethan says, "Well, every night before I get in bed with a woman, I whack my dick on the bedpost three times."

So the man decides to try it that very night. Before he climbs into bed, he whacks his dick on the bedpost three times.

His wife wakes up and says, "Ethan, is that you?"

Difficult Delivery

A man took his pregnant wife to the hospital. The doctor examined her and told them it would be a rather difficult delivery. He offered to let the couple try an experimental procedure. The woman would be connected to a machine that would transfer part of the pain to the father of the baby, thus reducing her own. The man quickly agreed.

The doctor warned him, though, that there was a slight bug in the machine that sometimes caused it to amplify the pain sent to the father, and if the pain became too much for to bear, he should let the doctor know immediately.

The doctor turned on the machine and watched the man. The man said he felt absolutely fine and he could take more. The doctor turned the dial up to 40, 60, 80, and finally 100% of the pain. The woman delivered the baby painlessly and the doctor stared at the man, astonished at how he could not even flinch with that much pain brought upon him. The couple took the new baby home.

There, on the front step, the mailman lay dead.

Old Friends

Two old friends, one rich and one poor, were sitting at a bar having a few drinks. After a while, they realize that both of their wedding anniversaries are the next day.

The poor man asks, "What did you get your wife for your wedding anniversary?"

The rich man replies, "I got her a red Ferrari and a diamond ring."

"Wow, what made you choose those gifts?"

The rich man, "I wasn't sure about the ring, so if she doesn't like it, she can take it back in her new car."

The poor man nods in agreement.

The rich man asks, "What did you get your wife?"

"I got her a pair of cheap slippers and a dildo."

The rich man asks, "Why did you choose those gifts?"

His poor friend responds, "Well, if she doesn't like the slippers, she can go fuck herself."

The Jewelry Store

A lady walks into a fancy jewelry store. She browses around, spots a beautiful diamond bracelet and walks over to inspect it. As she bends over to look more closely she inadvertently breaks wind.

Very embarrassed, she looks around nervously to see if anyone has noticed her little accident. As she turns around, her worst nightmare materializes in the form of a salesman standing right behind her.

Cool as a cucumber and displaying complete professionalism, the salesman greets the lady with, "Good day, Madam How may we help you today?"

Very uncomfortably, but hoping that the salesman may not have been there at the time of her little 'accident,' she asks, "Sir, what is the price of this lovely bracelet?"

He answers, "Madam, if you farted just looking at it, you're going to shit when I tell you the price."

The Egg Man

One day, while Sue was cleaning under the bed, she found a small box. Curious, she opened it and found three eggs and $10,000 in cash. Surprised and a little bit suspicious, she confronted her husband of twenty years about it.

"Oh, that," Frank said. "I felt a little guilty, so every time I cheated on you, I put an egg in this box."

Sue was a bit unhappy about this, but she figured that three affairs over twenty years wasn't so bad.

"But what about the $10,000?"

"Every time I got a dozen, I sold them."

The Good Doctor

"Doc, I think my son has VD," a patient told his urologist on the phone. "But the only woman he's screwed is our maid."

"Okay, don't be hard on him. He's just a kid," the doctor soothed, "Get him in here right away and I'll take care of him."

"But I've been screwing the maid too, and I've got the same symptoms he has."

"Then you come in with him and I'll fix you both up," replied the doctor.

"Well," the man admitted, "I think my wife has it too."

"Oh crap!" the physician roared, "That means we've all got it!"

The Peanut

Little Sally came home from school with a proud smile on her face.

She told her mom, "Frankie Jones showed me his willy today."

Before her mom had a chance to respond, Sally said, "It reminded me of a peanut."

With a little smile, her mom asked, "Was it really small?"

Sally replied, "No, really salty!"

The Mother-in-Law

A guy was standing in a bar when a stranger walks in. After a while they get to talking and drinking, and when he finally looks at his watch, he realizes it's 1 am.

"Oh man, I'm screwed. I better get home. My wife has told me a thousand times not to stay out this late."

The other guy replies, "I'll help you out of this. Just do what I say. Go home. Sneak into the bedroom. Pull back the covers. Get down between her legs then lick, lick and lick for about 20 minutes and there will be no complaints in the morning."

The guy agrees to try that and continues drinking with him for two more hours before heading home to give it a try. When he got home, the house was pitch black. He sneaks upstairs into the bedroom, pulls back the covers and proceeds to lick for 20 minutes. When he was done, he decided to wash his face. As he walked into the bathroom, his wife was sitting on the toilet.

Seeing her, he screamed, "What the hell are you doing in here?!"

"Quiet!" she exclaimed. "You'll wake my mother."

Dad Jokes

A father opens the door to his son's room and says, "Hey son, if you keep masturbating you're going to go blind."

His son responds, "Dad, I'm over here."

The Livestock

A man walks into his house with a duck under his arm.

He walks up to his wife and says, "This is the pig I've been fucking."

His wife says, "That's a duck, you dumbass."

He quickly replies, "I wasn't talking to you."

Burnt Toast

What do a slice of burnt toast and a pregnant girlfriend got in common?

In both cases, you wish you took it out a few seconds earlier.

The Peanuts

While watching TV with his wife, a man tosses peanuts into the air and catches them in his mouth. Just as he throws another peanut into the air, the front door opens, causing him to turn his head. The peanut falls into his ear and gets stuck.

His daughter comes in with her date. The man explains the situation, and the daughter's date says, "I can get the peanut out."

He tells the father to sit down, shoves two fingers into the father's nose, and tells him to blow hard. The father blows, and the peanut flies out of his ear.

After the daughter takes her date to the kitchen for something to eat, the mother turns to the father and says, "Isn't he smart? I wonder what he plans to be."

The father says, "From the smell of his fingers, I'd say our son-in-law."

The Mailman

Joe is on his last day at work as a mailman. He receives many thank-you cards and monetary gifts along his route. When he gets to the very last house, he's greeted by a gorgeous housewife who invites him in for lunch. Joe happily accepts.

After lunch, the woman invites him up to the bedroom for some "dessert." Joe happily accepts again.

When they are done, the woman hands him a dollar. Joe looks at her lying naked next to him and asks what the dollar is all about.

The woman replies: "It was my husband's suggestion. When I told him that it was your last day at work, he told me 'Screw him, give him a dollar.' The lunch was my idea."

The Island

After a shipwreck, a man is alone on a desert island. He manages to find food and build shelter, but he's lonely. And horny. After a while, he notices the wild goats high up on the mountain above him. He decides to catch one of the goats and keep it to satisfy his burning desires.

He weaves a rope out of jungle vines and spends day after day trying to capture a goat. After a month, he finally manages to lasso one and drag it back down the mountain.

He's pretty happy with himself and decides to try out his new goat. Unfortunately, the goat is not interested, and bucks and squirms and fights to get away, making a tremendous noise. No matter what the man does, he just can't get the goat to stay still long enough.

On the other side of the island, a woman who has long been stranded on the same desert island hears the noise and goes to investigate. She's shocked to see a man on the island! She been alone for months and needs a man desperately. She immediately tears off her palm leaf skirt and walks over to him as he attempts to wrestle the goat into position.

"Anything I can help you with?" she asks in her most flirtatious voice.

The man looks over, surprised to hear a human voice. He sees a naked woman, a vision of loveliness, in front of him.

"Anything?" he says, getting fairly excited.

"Yes, anything," she replies coquettishly.

So he says, "Will you hold this goat still for me?"

Italian Lover

An Italian guy is out picking up chicks in Rome. While at his favorite bar, he manages to attract one rather attractive blonde tourist. He takes her back to his place, and sure enough, they go at it.

After a long while, he climaxes loudly. Then he rolls over, lights up a cigarette and asks her, "So.... you finish?"

After a slight pause, she replies, "No."

Surprised, he puts out his cigarette, rolls back on top of her, and has his way with her again, this time lasting even longer than the first, and this time completing the deed with even louder shouts.

Again he rolls over, lights a cigarette, and asks, "So.... you finish?"

And again, after a short pause, she simply says, "No."

Stunned, but still acting reflexively on his macho pride, he once again puts out the cigarette, and mounts his companion du jour. This time, with all the strength he could muster up, he barely manages to end the task, but he does, after quite some time and energy is spent.

Barely able to roll over, he reaches for his cigarette, lights it again, and then asks tiredly, "So... you finish?"

"No. I'm Swedish."

The Affair

A doctor was having an affair with his nurse. One day, she told him she was pregnant. Not wanting his wife to know, he gave the nurse a sum of money and asked her to go to Italy and have the baby there.

"But how will I let you know the baby is born?" she asked.

He replied, "Just send me a postcard and write 'spaghetti' on the back. I'll take care of expenses."

Not knowing what else to do, the nurse took the money and flew to Italy. Six months went by, and then one day the doctor's wife called him at the office and said, "Dear, you received a very strange postcard in the mail today from Europe, and I don't understand what it means."

The doctor said, "Just wait until I get home and I will explain it to you."

Later that evening, the doctor came home, read the postcard, fell to the floor with a heart attack. Paramedics rushed him to the ER. The lead medic stayed back to comfort the wife. He asked what trauma had precipitated the cardiac arrest.

So the wife picked up the card and read, "'Spaghetti, Spaghetti, Spaghetti, Spaghetti. Two with sausage and meatballs, two without.'"

The Brothel

When we were visiting Las Vegas, my wife gave me permission to check out the legal brothels. I was pretty excited. The plane landed at 8 am, and I headed to a brothel immediately. I was in there like a flash and as I was the only client at that early hour, I had my choice of the girls.

I picked a gorgeous tall slim redhead, but before moving off to the room, she said that she won't work with anyone unless they are 10 inches long.

I was a little embarrassed and I asked her politely to sit back down. I mean, after all, no matter how hot the girl is, I'm not going to cut two inches of my manhood for anyone.

First Time

A man walks into a bar and says loudly, "Bartender, six shots!"

The bartender looks at him and says, "Wow six shots, what's the occasion?"

The man replies, "My first blowjob!"

The bartender then pours him a seventh shot and says, "Congrats man, this one's on me."

The man replies, "No thanks. If six shots can't get the taste out of my mouth, I don't know what will."

Statistically Speaking

Based a recent government survey, the most used sexual position among married couples is doggy style: the husband sits and begs, while the wife rolls over and plays dead.

Native Names

One day a tiny Apache Indian child walked into Big Chief Sitting Bull's Teepee.

"Sitting Bull," he asked, "Why does every man in our tribe have such long, complicated names?"

"Well," says Sitting Bull, "It's simple. Whenever a baby in this tribe is born, his Father wanders outside, absorbs the wonder of nature, and then names his child on the first thing he sees. Why do you ask, Two Dogs Fucking?"

Birds and Bees

A teenage girl come home from school and asks her mother, "Is it true what Rita just told me?"

"What's that?" asks her mother.

"That babies come out of the same place where boys put their penises?" said her daughter.

"Yes it is dear!" replies her mother, pleased that the subject had finally come up and that she wouldn't have to explain it to her daughter.

"But then, when I have a baby," responded the teenager, "won't it knock my teeth out?"

The Aliens

Two aliens landed in the Arizona desert near a gas station that was closed for the night.

They approached one of the gas pumps and the younger alien addressed it saying, "Greetings, Earthling. We come in peace. Take us to your leader."

The gas pump, of course, didn't respond. The younger alien became angry at the lack of response.

The older alien said, "I'd calm down if I were you."

The younger alien ignored the warning and repeated his greeting. Again, there was no response.

Annoyed by what he perceived to be the pump's arrogant attitude, he drew his ray gun and said impatiently, "Greetings, Earthling. We come in peace. Do not ignore us! Take us to your leader or I will fire!"

The older alien again warned his comrade saying, "You probably don't want to do that. I really don't think you should make him mad."

"Rubbish," replied the cocky young alien.

He aimed his weapon at the pump and opened fire. There was a huge explosion. A massive fireball roared towards them and blew the younger alien off his feet and deposited him a burnt, smoking mess about 200 yards away in a cactus patch. Half an hour passed. When he finally regained consciousness, he refocused his three eyes, straightened his bent antenna, and looked dazedly at the older, wiser alien who was standing over him shaking his big, green head.

"What a ferocious creature!" exclaimed the young, fried alien. "He nearly killed me! How did you know he was so dangerous?"

The older alien leaned over, placed a friendly feeler on his crispy friend and replied, "If there's one thing I've learned

during my intergalactic travels, you don't want to mess with a guy who can wrap his penis around himself twice and then stick it in his ear."

The Skunk

A couple driving home hit and wounded a skunk on the road. The wife gets out and brings it back to the car.

"We need to take it to a vet. Its shivering, it must be cold, what should I do?" she asks.

Husband replies "Put it between your legs to keep it warm."

"But it stinks!" she exclaims.

"So hold its nose!"

Three Nuns

In a terrible car accident, three nuns die at the same time. They all appear in front of the gates of Heaven to meet Saint Peter. When they arrive, Peter informs them that those who lived a life of the cloth must answer some basic questions about theology before they are permitted to enter Heaven.

Each of the nuns has studied their bible well, so they don't feel worried by this. The first nun steps forward and tells the saint that she's ready.

"Who was the first woman?" Peter asks.

"That's easy!" exclaims the nun. "Eve!"

Peter smiles, the bells toll, and the gates of Heaven open.

The second nun, encouraged by her colleague's easy pass, steps forwards and tells Peter that she's ready, as well.

"Who was the first man?" Peter asks.

"Easy! That's Adam!" says the nun, excitedly.

Peter smiles, the bells toll, and the gates of Heaven open.

The third nun is now confident that she won't have any trouble, and steps up to face Peter's question.

"What were Eve's first words to Adam?" he asks.

"My, that's a hard one," the nun replies worriedly, but Peter smiles, the bells toll, and the gates of Heaven open.

The Chicken Farmer

A woman walks into her accountant's office and tells him that she needs to file her taxes.

The accountant says, "Before we begin, I'll need to ask a few questions."

He gets her name, address, social security number, etc. and then asks, "What is your occupation?"

The woman replies, "I'm a whore."

The accountant balks and says, "No, no, no. That will never work. That is much too crass. Let's try to rephrase that."

The woman, "Ok, I'm a prostitute."

"No, that is still too crude. Try again."

They both think for a minute, and then the woman says, "I'm a chicken farmer."

The accountant asks, "What does chicken farming have to do with being a whore or a prostitute?"

"Well, I raised over 1,000 cocks last year."

The Sperm Bank

A masked man walks into a sperm bank and points his gun at the receptionist.

"I'm sorry, sir," the woman says, shaking in fear, "but this is a sperm bank. We don't have any money."

"Go to the vault and get a bottle," the man orders.

"OK, OK," the woman says nervously, "but this is sperm bank! There's no money!"

She returns with a jar full of semen.

"Open it," the man orders.

She slowly unscrews the top.

"Drink it," he orders.

"Drink it?" she asks, her knees shaking at the sight of the gun.

"Drink it!"

The woman tips the jar back and drinks the semen, swallowing every drop.

The man pulls off his mask and the receptionist recognizes her husband.

He says, "See, honey, its not that difficult, is it?"

The Optometrist

A man is at the optometrist getting his eyes checked.

"You need to stop masturbating," the optometrist says.

"Why?" asks the man. "Is it going to make me go blind?"

The optometrist looks around and says, "No, but it's making the other patients very uncomfortable."

The Fishermen

Two friends are fishing together, and one turns to the other and asks, "Is it rape if it's your wife?"

The second man cast his line and responded, "No, I don't think so."

"What a relief!" said the first man. "I thought you'd be mad as hell!"

Helpful Doctor

A married woman tells her doctor that her husband isn't interested in sex. They've tried Viagra and Cialis and every other drug, but they didn't help.

"Well, there is an experimental drug we could try, but it's very powerful," the doctor warned.

"Powerful is exactly what we need," she exclaimed happily.

The doctor gave her a bottle of pills and tells her to give them a try and then let him know how it's working.

"Remember, only one pill at a time," he says.

So she takes the pills home and puts one pill in her husband's dinner. That night, they make love for one hour. The next day, she's running around thrilled and happy.

"Oh, my God. I can't believe how well that worked," she thinks to herself.

That night she can't resist: she puts two pills in his food and that night they make love for two hours.

The next day, she's even more thrilled, so she dumps all the pills in his food.

Two weeks go by without any word from this woman, so the doctor decides to give her a call. A little boy answers the phone.

The doctor says, "Little boy, is your mother home?"

"No, she's... she's... who's this?" the little boy asks.

"I'm your mother's doctor and I gave her some pills to help her out a couple of weeks ago. Maybe you know how it's going?"

"That was you?!" the little boy says. "Let me tell you how it's going: Mom's dead, my sister's pregnant, my ass hurts, and Dad's in the attic going, 'Here kitty, kitty, kitty.'"

Shake It

Ben asks his new girlfriend for a hand job.

"I've never done that," the naïve girl says, "What do I do?"

"Well," replies Ben, "Remember when you were a kid and you'd shake a coke bottle and spray your brother with it? That's what you do."

She nods, so he pulls his manhood out and she grabs hold of it and starts shaking it. A minute later, he has tears running down his face, snot flowing from his nose, and wax flying from his ears.

She asks, "What's wrong?"

Ben cries "TAKE YOUR DAMN THUMB OFF THE END!"

Golf Pro

A famous American golfer is invited to go to China for a golfing tournament. From the second he gets there, he is treated like a king. He is given five-star treatment in a five-star hotel until the day of the tournament. The night before the tournament, he is sitting in his hotel room watching TV.

A hot Chinese girl knocks on his door. He takes one look at her and says to himself, 'Wow. They must really love me here.'

He takes her to bed, but almost immediately, she yells, "Chung Hoi!"

The golfer is pretty proud of himself, making a young girl scream like that. She continues to scream, "Chung Hoi! Chung Hoi!," all night long.

At the tournament the next day, the American golfer gets a hole-in-one and gets really excited. He starts yelling, "Chung Hoi! Chung Hoi!"

One of the Chinese golfers says, "What do you mean 'WRONG HOLE'?"

Nude Beach

A father, mother, and son were going to Europe and were planning to visit the nude beaches while they were there. They didn't want the son to get a distorted view of beauty, so they told him, "The men with really big dicks and the girls with really, really big boobs were both really, really dumb."

When they got to the beach they split up. Later the mother saw the son and asked where his dad was.

The boy said, "Well, the last time I saw him he was talking to this really, really, dumb blonde, and the longer they talked, the dumber he got."

Secret Code

A husband and wife have small children, so they decide to make a password for sex so they cold speak in front of the kids. They decide on 'washing machine'.

In bed one night, husband says, "Washing machine."

His wife replies, "Not tonight, darling, I have a headache."

Half an hour passes and she feels guilty so she says, "Washing machine."

Her husband replies, "Too late; it was only a small load so I decided to do it by hand."

Size Large

A woman walks into a drugstore and asks the pharmacist if he sells size extra large condoms.

He replies, "Yes we do. Would you like to buy some?"

She responds, "No sir, but do you mind if I wait around here until someone does?"

The Bieber

A girlfriend and boyfriend walked into the girlfriend's house and the girl said to her mom, "Mom, me and my boyfriend are going up to my room."

Her mom says, "Ok honey, you kids have fun."

While they are up there, the mom hears: "Baby baby baby oh!"

The mom walks to the door and asks, "What the hell is going on in there?"

The girl says, "Mom, we're just having sex."

The mom replies, "Oh thank God -- I thought you guys were listening to Justin Bieber."

The Sperm Bank

A man and a woman meet in an elevator.

"Where are you heading today?" the man asks.

"I'm going down to give blood."

"How much do you get paid for giving blood?"

"About $20."

"Wow," says the man, "I'm going up to donate sperm, and the sperm bank pays $100."

The woman angrily gets off the elevator. The next day, the man and woman meet in the elevator again.

"Fancy meeting you again. Where you off to today?"

The woman just shakes her head.

"I'm sorry, where are you headed?" the man asked, confused.

She shakes her head again.

The man repeat the question, "Where to?"

Finally, he hears her mumble, "sperm bank," with her mouth full.

The Prescription

A man went to the doctor's office to get prescription for a double dose of Viagra. The doctor told him that he couldn't allow him a double dose.

"Why not?" asked the man.

"Because it's not safe," replied the doctor.

"But I need it really bad," said the man.

"Well, why do you need it so badly?" asked the doctor.

The man said, "My girlfriend is coming into town on Friday; my ex-wife will be here on Saturday; and my wife is coming home on Sunday. Can't you see? I must have a double dose."

The doctor finally relented saying, "Okay, I'll give it to you, but you have to come in on Monday morning so that I can check you to see if there are any side effects."

On Monday, the man dragged himself in with his arm in a sling.

The doctor asked, "What happened to you?"

The man said, "No one showed up."

The Elephant

A couple took their young son for his first visit to the circus.

When his father left to buy popcorn, the boy asked, "Mom, what's that long thing on the elephant?"

"That's the elephant's trunk, dear," she replied.

"No, Mom, down underneath."

His mother blushed and said, "Oh, that's nothing."

The father returned, and the mother went off to get a soda. As soon as she left, the boy repeated his question.

The father took a good look and explained, "That's the elephant's penis."

"Dad, how come when I asked Mom, she said it was nothing?"

The man took a deep breath and replied, "Son, I've spoiled that woman."

The Train Conductor

A man in Bulgaria drove trains for a living. He loved his job. Driving a train had been his dream ever since he was a child. He loved to make the train go as fast as possible.

Unfortunately, one day he was a little too reckless and caused a crash. He made it out, but a passenger died.

Well, needless to say, he went to court over this incident. He was found guilty, and was sentenced to death by electrocution.

When the day of the execution came, he requested a single banana as his last meal. After eating the banana, he was strapped into the electric chair. The switch was flown, sparks flew, and smoke filled the air - but nothing happened. The man was perfectly fine.

Well, at the time, there was an old Bulgarian law that said a failed execution was a sign of divine intervention, so the man was allowed to go free.

Somehow, he managed to get his old job back driving the train. Having not learned his lesson at all, he went right back to driving the train with reckless abandon.

Once again, he caused a train to crash, this time killing two people. The trial went much the same as the first, resulting in a sentence of execution. For his final meal, the man requested two bananas. After eating the bananas, he was strapped into the electric chair. The switch was thrown, sparks flew, smoke filled the room - and the man was once again unharmed.

Well, this of course meant that he was free to go. And once again, he somehow managed to get his old job back. To what should have been the surprise of no one, he crashed yet another train and killed three people. And so he once again found himself being sentenced to death. On the day of his execution, he requested his final meal: three bananas.

"You know what? No," said the executioner. "I've had it with you and your stupid bananas and walking out of here unharmed. I'm not giving you a thing to eat; we're strapping you in and doing this now."

Well, it was against protocol, but the man was strapped in to the electric chair without a last meal. The switch was pulled, sparks flew, smoke filled the room - and the man was still unharmed. The executioner was speechless.

The man looked at the executioner and said, "Oh, the bananas had nothing to do with it. I'm just a bad conductor."

The License

A man named Jed went hunting near the border of Alabama and Georgia. When he was going back to his truck, a game warden came up to him and asked him what he had in the sack.

"Three rabbits," Jed said.

The warden said, "Let me see one of those rabbits."

So Jed pulled out one of the rabbits. The warden stuck his finger in the rabbit's butthole, pulled it out, smelled it and said, "This is a Georgia rabbit."

Then the warden said, "Let me see your Georgia huntin' license."

So Jed showed him. Then the warden said, "Let me see another one of those rabbits." So Jed pulled out another rabbit.

Then the warden stuck his finger in the rabbit's bunghole, tasted it and said, "This is a Alabama rabbit. Let me see your Alabama huntin' license."

So Jed showed it to him.

Then the game warden said, "Where you from boy?"

So Jed pulled his pants down and said, "You figure it out!"

Herding Goats

An Islamic terrorist decided to leave the battlefield and return to his ancestors' traditional way of life: herding goats. He got himself a small herd of goats in the mountains of Afghanistan, but he didn't know what he was doing.

An old man led his herd of goats down a trail by the young man's herd and advised him, "If you tie a bell around your lead goat, you'll always know where he is."

The young man tried it, and it worked. Day after day, the old man would give the young man advice. The young man liked his new lifestyle, but he was lonely. He decided to ask the old man for advice on this, too.

"Don't you ever get lonely," the young man asked the old man, "alone on the mountain with your goats?"

"Of course," the old man nodded. "We all do. Here's what you do: take one of your goats and tie her to a tree. Then, have your way with her."

"Really?" asked the young terrorist dubiously.

"Yes," said the old man.

After a few more lonely days, the young terrorist couldn't resist. He tied one of his young goats to a tree, stood behind her, and began to have his way with her.

Just then, the old man and several other goat herders came down the trail and saw the young man and his goat. They all started laughing hysterically and slapping their thighs.

"You said everyone did it with their goats!" the young man complained.

"Yeah, but not the ugly ones!" the old man laughed.

The Marine

By the time a Marine pulled into a little town, every hotel room was taken.

"You've got to have a room somewhere," he pleaded. "Or just a bed, I don't care where."

"Well, I do have a double room with one occupant, a Navy guy," admitted the manager, "and he might be glad to split the cost. But to tell you the truth, he snores so loudly that people in adjoining rooms have complained in the past. I'm not sure it'd be worth it to you."

"No problem," the tired Marine assured him. "I'll take it."

The next morning the Marine came down to breakfast bright-eyed and bushy-tailed.
"How'd you sleep?" asked the manager.

"Never better."

The manager was impressed.

"No problem with the other guy snoring, then?"

"Nope, I shut him up in no time," said the Marine.

"How'd you manage that?" asked the manager.

"He was already in bed, snoring away, when I came in the room," the Marine explained. "I went over, gave him a kiss on the cheek, and said, 'Goodnight, beautiful,' and he sat up all night watching me."

The Vegas Girl

A man on a business trip to Las Vegas heard that the Las Vegas prostitutes were amazing. On his first night there, he decided he would go out and try his luck. He walked outside his hotel and looked up and down the street and saw an attractive girl standing on the corner.

He approached her and asked if she was working and, sure enough, she said, "Sure, let's go to my room."

He was in luck. She was a knockout. They got to the room and he sat down anxiously on the edge of the bed.

She asked him what he wanted and he thought for a second, and then said "How much for a hand job?"

She said, "$300".

His eyes popped open and he asked "$300? For a hand job?"

She said, "Walk over to that window and open the curtains. See that motel down there? I own it, and I didn't inherit it. I'm that good."

He said, "Well, OK, go right ahead, honey".

So she proceeded to give him the best hand job he ever had. After a little rest he asked, "How much for a blow job?"

She said "$600".

"$600? OH MY GOD!" he replied.

She told him to walk back over to the window. "See that 15 story hotel? I own it and I didn't inherit it. I'm that good."

He said, "Well, get to work then, sweetie."

And sure enough he got the best blow job he ever received.

After a little recovery time, he asked, "How much for sex?"

She chuckled and said, "Honey, if I had a pussy I'd own this whole damned town."

The Smoker

Two older women were outside their nursing home, having a smoke, when it started to rain. One of the ladies pulled out a condom, cut off the end, put it over her cigarette, and continued smoking.

The first lady asked, "Whats that?"

The second old lady responded, "A condom. This way my cigarette doesn't get wet."

"Where did you get it?"

"You can get them at any drugstore."

The next day, the old lady hobbles herself into the local drugstore and announces to the pharmacist that she wants a box of condoms. The guy, obviously embarrassed, looks at her strangely (she is, after all, over 80 years old), but very delicately asks what brand she prefers.

"Doesn't matter, son, as long as it fits a Camel," she said.

Funny Smell

A guy walks into an elevator and stands next to a beautiful woman.

After a few minutes he turns to her and says, "Can I smell your pussy?"

The woman looks at him in disgust and says, "Certainly not!"

"Hmmm," he replies. "It must be your feet, then."

Fishing Trip

One bright sunny morning, a man turns to his lovely wife and says, "Wife, we're going fishing this weekend, you, me and the dog."

The wife complains, "But I don't like fishing!"

"Look! We're going fishing, and that's final."

"Do I have to go fishing with you? I really don't want to go!"

"I'll give you three choices: you come fishing with me and the dog, you give me a blow job, or you take it up the ass!"

The wife grimaces, "But I don't want to do any of those things!"

"Wife, I've given you three options, and you're going to have to do one of them. I'm going to the garage to sort out my fishing tackle, when I come back I expect you to have made up your mind!"

The wife sits and thinks about it.

Twenty minutes later her husband comes back, "Well! What have you decided? Fishing with me and the dog, blow job, or ass?"

The wife complains some more and finally makes up her mind, "OK, OK, I'll give you a blow job!"

"Great!" He says and drops his pants.

The wife is on her knees doing the business.

Suddenly she stops, looks up at her husband and says, "Oh! It tastes absolutely disgusting! It tastes all shitty!"

"Yeah," says her husband, "The dog didn't want to go fishing either."

The Anthropologist

A Harvard professor of anthropology is on a six-month research trip to the middle of the unexplored Amazonian rain forest to study remote tribes. He's been alone in the jungle for months and he's lonely.

On a visit with an Indian tribe full of men, he asks, "How do you guys relieve your sexual tension?"

"Simple, just come down to the river tomorrow and we'll show you."

The next day the professor shows up and sees a group of men near a donkey.

One man says, "Since you're our guest, you get to go first."

The professor, careful not to offend the tribesmen by refusing their custom, then proceeds to have sex with the donkey.

After a few minutes watching the professor screwing the donkey, a man in the group asks, "Are you almost done, professor? We need the donkey to cross the river in order to get to the tribe of women."

The Undercover Cop

A man tells his friend at a bar about the new girl he met.

"I've been chatting with her online. She's fourteen-years-old, but she's so mature for her age! She's funny, sexy, and flirty."

"Wow, says his friend. "Surprising to meet a girl that young who's so mature."

"Yeah," the man nods. "And now she tells me she's an undercover cop. How cool is that at her age!"

The Robbery

A man was getting ready to close his bar for the night when a robber with a ski mask burst in and pulls a gun.

He yells to him, "This is a stick-up! Put all your dough in this bag!"

The scared the man pleads, "Don't shoot, please! I'll do as you say!"

The robber yells, "Shut up and empty the cash register!"

"Okay, okay! Just don't shoot, I have a wife and kids! I'll do whatever you say!"

The crook takes the money then puts the gun to the man's head and says, "Alright, now give me a blowjob!"

"Anything!" the man cries, "Just don't shoot!"

The man starts to blow the crook. As the crook gets excited, he drops the gun.

The man sees the gun on the floor, picks it up, hands it back to the crook and says, "Hold the gun, damn it! Somebody might walk in!"

Three Babies

Three babies in the womb discuss what they would like to be when they grow up.

The first one says, "I wanna be a plumber, so I can fix the pipes in here."

The second one says, "I wanna be an electrician, so I can have some light in here."

The third one says, "I wanna be a boxer."

The others look confused and ask, "Why do you want to be a boxer?"

He angrily replies, "So I can beat the hell out of that rude bald guy who keeps coming in here and spitting on us."

Widdle Wabbits

An adorable little girl walks into a pet shop and asks in the sweetest little lisp, "Excuthe me, mithter, do you keep widdle wabbits?"

As the shopkeeper's heart melts, he gets down on his knees, so that he's on her level, and asks, "Do you want a widdle white wabby or a thoft and fuwwy back wabby or maybe one like that cute widdle bwown wabby over there?"

She, in turn blushes, rocks on her heels, puts her hands on her knees, leans forward and says in a quiet voice, "I don't fink my pet python weally gives a thit."

The Taxi

One day a nun was standing on the side of the road waiting for a cab. A cab stopped and picked her up. During the ride she noticed that the driver was staring at her.

When she asked him why, he said, "I want to ask you something, but I don't want to offend you."

She said, "You can't offend me. I have been a nun long enough that I have heard just about everything."

The cab driver then said, "Well, I've always had a fantasy to have a nun give me a blow job."

She said, "Well, perhaps we can work something out under two conditions: you have to be single, and you have to be Catholic."

Immediately the cab driver said, "Oh, yes! I'm single and I'm Catholic!"

The nun said, "Okay, pull into that alley."

The cab driver pulled into the alley and the nun went to work.

Shortly afterwards, the cab driver started crying.

The nun said, "My child, what's the matter?"

He said tearfully, "Sister, I have sinned. I lied, I lied. I'm married and I'm Jewish!"

The nun replied, "That's okay. My name's Bruce and I'm on my way to a costume party!"

The Voodoo That You Do

There was a businessman who was getting ready to go on a long business trip. He knew his wife was a flirtatious sort, so he thought he'd try to get her something to keep her occupied while he was gone, because he didn't much like the idea of her screwing someone else. So he went to a store that sold sex toys and started looking around.

He thought about a life-sized sex doll, but that was too close to another man for him. He was browsing through the dildos, looking for something special to please his wife, and started talking to the old man behind the counter. He explained his situation, the old man.

"Well, I don't really know of anything that will do the trick. We have vibrating dildos, special attachments, and so on, but I don't know of anything that will keep her occupied for weeks, except ..." said the old man, and then he stopped.

"Except what?" asked the businessman.

"Nothing, nothing," said the old man.

"C'mon, tell me! I need something!" protested the businessman.

"Well, sir, I don't usually mention this, but there is the 'voodoo dick,'" the old man said.

"Voodoo dick? What's a voodoo dick?" the businessman asked.

The old man reached under the counter, and pulled out an old wooden box carved with strange symbols. He opened it, and there lie a very ordinary-looking dildo.

The businessman laughed, and said, "Big fucking deal. It looks like every other dildo in this shop!"

The old man said, "But you haven't seen what it'll do yet."

He pointed to a door and said "Voodoo dick, the door."

The voodoo dick rose out of its box, darted over to the door, and started screwing the keyhole. The whole door shook with the vibrations, and a crack developed down the middle.

Before the door could split, the old man said, "Voodoo dick, get back in your box!"

The voodoo dick stopped, floated back to the box, and lay there, quiet once more.

The businessman said, "I'll take it!"

The old man resisted and said it wasn't for sale, but he finally surrendered to $2,000 in cash.

The guy took it home to his wife, told her it was a special dildo and that to use it, all she had to do was say, "Voodoo dick, my pussy."

He left for his trip satisfied things would be fine while he was gone. After he'd been gone a few days, the wife was unbearably horny. She thought of several people who would willingly satisfy her, but then she remembered the voodoo dick.

She got it out, and said "Voodoo dick, my pussy!"

The voodoo dick shot to her crotch and started pumping. It was great, like nothing she'd ever experienced before. After three orgasms, she decided she'd had enough, and tried to pull it out, but it was stuck in her, still thrusting. She tried and tried to get it out, but nothing worked. Her husband had forgot to tell her how to shut it off. So she decided to go to the hospital to see if they could help.

She put her clothes on, got in the car and started to drive to the hospital, quivering with every thrust of the dildo. On the way, another orgasm nearly made her swerve off the road, and she was pulled over by a policeman. He asked for her license, and then asked how much she'd had to drink.

Gasping and twitching, she explained that she hadn't been drinking, but that a voodoo dick was stuck in her pussy, and wouldn't stop screwing her.

The officer looked at her for a second, and then said, "Yeah, right. Voodoo dick, my ass!"

The Fan

After several years of marriage, a husband asked his wife, "Honey, do you have any fantasies that I can fulfill?"

"Well," said the wife to her husband, "I do have this one fantasy that we're making love while an African servant stands beside the bed and waves a fan over our naked writhing bodies. I think it would really turn me on."

The husband decided to make the dream come true, so he found a black man and offered him $200 to wave a fan over them while they made love. The three of them went home and the couple started having sex while the black man was waving the fan.

But the wife complained that she couldn't get any satisfaction, so she proposed that they should change roles. She would make love with the black man and the husband would wave the fan over them.

The husband agreed and started waving the fan. After a while, the wife moaned with pleasure and begged for more as the black man plowed her from behind.

So the husband said to the black man: "Now do you understand how you should wave the fan, you jackass?"

The Navy

A man joins the navy and is shipped out immediately to an aircraft carrier in the middle of the Pacific Ocean. The captain is showing the new recruit around the ship, when the recruit asks the captain what the sailors do to satisfy their urges when they're at sea for so long.

"Let me show you," says the captain.

He takes the recruit down to the rear of the ship where there's a solitary barrel with a hole in it.

"This'll be the best sex you'll ever have. Go ahead and try it, and I'll give you some privacy."

The recruit doesn't quite believe it, but he decides to try it anyway. He checks to see if anyone is looking, and then sticks his business in the hole. After he finishes up, the captain returns.

"Wow! That was the best sex I've ever had! I want to do it every day!"

"Fine. You can do it every day except for Thursday."

"Why not Thursday?"

"That's your day in the barrel."

The Raffle Ticket

A woman arrives home from work and her husband notices she's wearing a diamond necklace.

He asks his wife, "Where did you get that necklace?"

She replies, "I won it in a raffle at work. Go get my bath ready while I start dinner."

The next day, the woman arrives home from work wearing a diamond bracelet.

Her husband asks, "Where did you get the bracelet?"

She replies, "I won it in a raffle at work. Go get my bath ready while I start dinner."

The next day, her husband notices she arrives home from work wearing a mink coat.

He says, "I suppose you won that in a raffle at work?"

She replies, "Yeah I did! How did you guess? Go get my bath ready while I start supper."

Later, after supper, she goes to take her bath and she notices there is only one inch of water in the tub.

She yells to her husband, "HEY! There's only an inch of water in the tub."

He replies, "I didn't want you to get your raffle ticket wet."

The Gorilla

A woman and her friend are visiting the zoo. They are standing in front of the big silverback gorilla's cage when one woman makes a gesture that the gorilla interprets as an invitation. He grabs her, yanks her over the fence, and takes her to his nest in the pen.

There he ravishes her and makes passionate love to her for about two hours until he is tranquilized, and the lady is rescued. The lady is taken to hospital to recover. Her friend, deeply concerned, visits her the next day.

"Are you hurt?" she asks.

The lady replies, "Of course I'm hurt! He hasn't called! He hasn't texted!"

Hotel Porn

A family walks into a hotel and as the father is checking in, he says quietly to the desk clerk, "I hope the porn is disabled."

The guy at the desk replies. "It's just regular porn, you sick bastard."

The Ladder to Success

One day, Harry came upon a big, long ladder that stretched into the clouds. He'd walked this way every day and this ladder was never there before. Curious and brave, he began to climb.

Eventually, he climbed into the layer of clouds, and saw a rather large, homely woman lying there on a cloud.

She said, "Take me now or climb the ladder to success!"

Harry figured success had to be better than this, so he continued climbing. He came upon another level of clouds, and found a thinner, cuter woman than before.

She said to him, "Take me now or climb the ladder to success!"

Harry saw that his luck was changing and so continued his climb. On another level of clouds, he found a rather attractive woman with not so bad of a figure.

She said, "Take me now or climb the ladder to success!"

Harry really liked his chances now! He climbed quickly and deftly, and sure enough, on the next level, he found a gorgeous, lithe, well-endowed woman lying seductively on the cloud.

"Take me now or climb the ladder to success," she whispered seductively.

Harry couldn't believe his eyes, but his greed caught the best of him. He climbed to the next level, expecting to find a supermodel.

Suddenly, the ladder ends, and a latch closes behind him. He looks over to see a 400-pound, 6'8", hairy, dirty, biker-looking guy with tattoos. The biker gets up and walks menacingly toward Harry.

Apprehensively, Harry whispers, "Who are you?"

The biker answers, "I'm Cess."

The Martians

One day, a space ship landed in a farmer's field and a Martian man and his wife got out and introduced themselves to the farmer and his wife. As a token of his friendship, the farmer immediately invited the Martian couple in his home and begged them to stay for the evening and have dinner, so the Martians agreed.

Later that night, the Martian man explained how, on their planet, it was customary to swap partners as a token of friendship. The farmer, not wanting to offend his alien neighbors, readily agreed. The Martian then man took the farmer's wife into one bedroom while the farmer took the Martian woman into another.

They had been having sex for about an hour when the Martian man asked the farmer's wife, "Well, how do you like having sex with a Martian? How does it feel?"

The farmer's wife replied, "Well, I wish it was a little longer."

So the Martian man twisted his right ear and presto, his penis became longer.

About an hour later, the Martian man asked the farmer's wife again "How does it feel now?"

he farmer's wife responded, "I think it needs to be a little thicker."

The Martian man twisted his left ear and presto, his penis became thicker.

The next morning, after their alien neighbors had left, the farmer and his wife were having coffee at the breakfast table.

The farmer asked his wife, "How was the Martian man?"

To this, the farmer's wife replied, "Fine. And how about the Martian woman?"

The farmer replied, "Hated it. She yanked on my ears all night long!"

Elderly Art

Two old ladies are walking through a museum and got separated.

When they ran into each other later the first old lady said to the second, "Oh my! Did you see that statue of the naked man back there?"

The second old lady replied, "Yes! I was absolutely shocked! How can they display such a thing! My gosh, the penis on it was so large!"

Where upon the first old lady accidentally blurted out, "Yeah, and cold, too!"

The Virgin

A rich forty-year-old American woman decided to get married, but she wanted her husband to be a virgin like her. After some years of fruitless searching, she hadn't found anyone who met the description and decided to try an online dating service.

A month later, she was connected with an Australian man who had never been with a woman in his life and she married him immediately. On the night of their wedding, she went to the bathroom to freshen up and then went back to the bedroom, happy to be with her virgin husband.

When she entered the bedroom, she saw her husband standing naked in the center of the room and all the furniture pushed into one corner of the room.

"What happened?" asked the surprised woman.

"Look, I've never been with a woman, but if it's the same as with a kangaroo, then I'll need the whole room to catch you!"

The Wish

One day a man walked into the bar with a cat on his shoulder, not just any cat, but the sweetest-looking little ginger kitten. But that wasn't the weirdest thing; a six-foot ostrich with eyes like baseballs followed them in - a real live ostrich!

I asked the man what he wanted.

"I'll have a beer," he said. "And a beer for the ostrich and a gin and tonic for the cat."

The cat meowed and licked his paw. So cute.

"Make that a double gin and tonic, please," the cat said adorably. "Thanks."

I was astonished.

Well, I served the drinks, he paid, and they all knocked 'em back. It wasn't long before the ostrich came back to the bar, and made it clear that he wanted the same again. Well, I poured them.

I could feel the cat's angelic eyes on me as if he was checking that he got his double again. I took the drinks over to them, and the man paid, taking the cash from a purse tied around the ostrich's neck. This went on for a couple of hours. The man and the ostrich buying alternate rounds, while the cat just sat on the window shelf with his drink, looking adorable.

The whole place got quiet. People sat and stared, and who could blame them? Eventually, I plucked up the courage to ask the fellow just what was going on.

"Can't a man have a quiet drink anymore?" he grumbled.

So I said, "No offense, but you've got to admit that you're a unique set of drinkers."

He smiled, but there was no light in that smile.

"Okay, you really want to know? I'll tell you. I was on a job across town the other week, working on the new road. As we dug, I saw something shiny, and I stopped my backhoe to take a look, and it turned out to be this old brass lamp. I rubbed it, thinking there might be a date or inscription or something on it. Anyway, out comes this cloud of smoke and a Genie appeared. You know, with a turban, a scimitar, and the whole works. And he tells me I've got just one wish."

The man paused and took a sip of his beer.

"And before you ask, yes, I did wish for a long-legged bird with a sweet pussy. But this wasn't what I had in mind."

The Gator

A Cajun guy walks into a bar with an alligator under his arm. He asks the bartender if he will give him free drinks if he shows he can put his penis inside the alligator's mouth for 15 seconds without it getting bit off.

The bartender agrees, "This I've got to see!"

The Cajun opens the alligator's mouth and puts his penis inside it; the alligator gently closes his mouth. The Cajun stands there for 15 seconds with the whole bar holding their breath.

Finally, the Cajun hits the alligator over the head a bottle, causing the alligator to open his mouth and let the guy withdraw his penis. The bar cheers!

The bartender starts serving the free drinks to the Cajun and then tells everyone in the bar "If anyone else can do that, I'll give them free drinks too!"

There is a pause and then a Texan in the back wearing his boots and cowboy hat calls out, "OK, I'll do it, but please don't hit me so hard with the bottle".

The Afterlife

A couple made a deal that whoever died first would come back and inform the other of the afterlife. After a long life, the husband was the first to go, and, true to his word, he made contact.

A ghostly spectre appeared in their bedroom at night and said, "Mary. Mary."

"Is that you, Fred?"

"Yes, I've come back like we agreed."

"What's it like?"

"Well, I get up in the morning, I have sex, I have breakfast, off to the golf course, I have sex, I bathe in the sun, and then I have sex twice. I have lunch, another romp around the golf course, then sex pretty much all afternoon. After supper, golf course again. Then have sex until late at night. The next day it starts again."

"Oh, Fred you surely must be in heaven."

"Not exactly. I'm a rabbit."

The Hill-top

A kid walks into a class with a muddy shirt and missing his socks and shoes.

His teacher asks, "Where have you been?"

The boy says, "On top of blueberry hill."

Then another boy walks in with no shirt and no shoes and the teacher says, "Where have you been?"

The boy says, "On top of blueberry hill."

Then a girl walks in wearing a muddy, torn dress, and the teacher says, "Let me guess: you were on top of blueberry hill."

The girl responds, "No, I am Blueberry Hill."

Sound Sleeper

Two married buddies were out drinking one night when one turns to the other and says, "You know, I don't know what else to do. Whenever I go home after we've been out drinking, I turn the headlights off before I get to the driveway. I shut off the engine and coast into the garage. I take my shoes off before I go into the house, I sneak up the stairs, I get undressed in the bathroom. I ease into bed and my wife still wakes up and yells at me for staying out so late!"

His buddy looks at him and says, "Well, you're obviously taking the wrong approach. I screech into the driveway, slam the door, storm up the steps, throw my shoes into the closet, jump into bed, rub my hands on my wife's ass and say, 'How about a blowjob?' and she's always sound asleep."

Finishing the Job

A wife says to her husband, "You make love like you mow the lawn."

Husband replies, proud of himself, "You mean very slowly and professionally?"

"No," she replies, "I mean I have to finish the job myself."

The Restroom

I took my kid to the baseball game, and after a large soda, he needed to use the bathroom. Between innings, I took him to the very crowded public restroom.

After looking to the man using the urinal to his right, my six-year-old son turns to me on his left and exclaims, "Daddy, that man's wiener is a lot bigger than yours!"

The whole bathroom heard and looked immediately at me, laughing.

So I put my hand on my kid's shoulder and told him, "Well, son, that's because daddy isn't aroused by men."

The Spaghetti

A guy orders spaghetti in a restaurant. In the middle of eating, he finds a hair in his food.

He says to the waiter, "I'm not paying for this dirty meal," and walks out.

The waiter watches the guy leave, walk across the street, and go into the whorehouse across the street. The waiter waits about ten minutes, bursts through the door and finds the guy with his face buried in pussy.

The waiter says, "You complain about one hair in your spaghetti, and you come over here and eat that?"

The man replies, "Yeah, and if I find any spaghetti in this pussy, I'm not paying for it either."

Nice Hair

Every day, a male co-worker walks up very close to a lady at the coffee machine, inhales a big breath of air and tells her that her hair smells nice. After a week of this, she can't stand it anymore, and takes her complaint to a Supervisor in the HR department and asks to file a sexual harassment grievance against him.

The Human Resources supervisor is puzzled, and asks: "What's threatening about a co-worker telling you your hair smells nice?"

"It's Ralph," explains the woman. "Ralph the midget?"

The Grandmother

A woman and baby are in the pediatrician's office. The doctor is concerned about the baby's weight and asks, "Is he bottle fed or breast fed?"

The woman replies, "Breast fed."

The doctor has her to strip down to her waist so he can examine her breasts. He pinches her nipples and massages and rubs both breasts for a while.

"No wonder the baby is underweight, you have no milk."

The woman replies, "I know, I'm his grandmother. But I'm glad I came!"

The Hairy Chest

Two gay lovers, Allen and Nate, are lying in bed together when Allen starts rubbing vaseline on his chest.

Nate asks, "What you doing?""

Rupert replies, "I read that vaseline stimulates hair growth and I want a hairy chest."

Nate laughs, "Don't be stupid! If that was true, I would have a ponytail sticking out of my ass."

The Ghost

At a conference on the supernatural, one of the speakers asked, "Who here has ever seen a ghost?"

Most of the hands go up.

"And how many of you have had some form of interaction with a ghost?"

About half the hands stay up.

"Okay, now how many of you have had physical contact with a ghost?"

Three hands stay up; there's a slight murmur in the crowd.

"Gosh, that's pretty good. Okay, have any of you ever, uh, well, been intimate with a ghost?"

One hand stays up. The speaker blinks.

"Gosh, sir, are you telling us that you've actually had sexual contact with a ghost?"

The fellow suddenly blushes and says, "Oh, I'm sorry... I thought you said goat!"

Getting Old

Three old men were sitting around talking about who had the worst health problems.

The seventy-year-old said, "Have I got a problem. Every morning I get up at 7:30 and have to take a piss, but I have to stand at the toilet for an hour 'cause my pee barely trickles out."

"Heck, that's nothing, " said the eighty year old. "Every morning at 8:30 I have to take a shit, but I have to sit on the can for hours because of my constipation. It's terrible".

The ninety-year-old said, "You guys think you have problems! Every morning at 7:30, I piss like a racehorse, and at 8:30 I shit like a pig."

"What's wrong with that?" the other two men ask.

"The trouble is, I don't wake up till eleven."

The Boyfriend

A girl was talking to her mother about her concern about her new boyfriend. The boyfriend had been in an accident.

"He's sweet, he has a great job, he takes great care of me," the girl said, "but I'm just not sure I can stay with him.

"So what's wrong with him?" her mother asked.

"Well, he only has one foot," the girl said.

Her mother sighed into the phone and said, "Dear, that's nothing to worry about. Your father only has five inches!"

The Marriage

A man comes home and asks his wife to tell him something that is going to make him laugh and cry.

His wife thinks for a minute and says, "Of all your friends, you have the biggest dick."

Wet Girl

My girlfriend screamed at me, "Give it to me! I'm dripping wet!"

She shouted again, "Give it to me now! I'm soaking fucking wet!"

I don't care how much she shouts; I'm not giving her the umbrella.

The Anniversary

A man and his wife return to their honeymoon hotel for their 25th anniversary.

As the couple reflected on that magical evening twenty-five years ago, the wife asked the husband, "When you first saw my naked body in front of you, what was going through your mind?"

The husband replied, "All I wanted to do was to screw your brains out and suck your tits dry."

Then, as the wife undressed, she asked, "What are you thinking now?"

He replied, "It looks like I did a pretty good job."

War is Hell

During a war, a soldier entered a recently conquered village and lined up all the women.

The soldier shouted at the women, "I'm going to rape all of you if you don't tell me where the weapons are hidden!"

A trembling young lady said to the soldier bravely, "Rape us if you must, but please spare our grandmother!"

The grandmother looked at the strapping young soldier and said to her granddaughter, "Shut up, war is war."

The Vibrator

An old woman goes in to a sex shop, shaking.

"Sir," she says in a shaky voice, "do you sell vibrators?"

"Yes, ma'am."

"And are they this big around and this long?" she asks in a shaky voice, holding her hands about six inches apart.

"Yes, ma'am."

"And they're $22.95?" she asks in a shaky voice.

"Yes, ma'am," the salesman nods. "We carry those."

"How do you turn them off?"

The Retirement Home

After living in the same retirement home for months, octogenarian Frank and septuagenarian Jane's romance blossomed. One day after bingo, they seized the opportunity to sneak into a supply closet to consummate their lust.

Frank finds Jane very tight and difficult to enter, but finally succeeds.

When they are finished, Frank says to her, "If I had known you were a virgin, I would have been more gentle!"

To which Jane replies, "If I'd known you could get an erection, I would have taken off my pantyhose!"

The Stripper

Dating a stripper is like eating a noisy bag of chips in a movie theater: everyone looks at you in disgust, but deep down inside they want some too.

The Gynecologist

During an international gynecological conference, an English doctor, Dr. Betts, and a French doctor, Dr. Bernard, were discussing unusual cases they had treated recently.

"Only last week," Dr. Bernard said, "a woman came to see me with a clitoris like a melon!"

"Don't be absurd," Dr. Betts exclaimed, "It couldn't have been that big. My God, man, she wouldn't be able to walk if it were."

"Aah, you English, always thinking about size," replied Dr. Bernard. "I was talking about the flavor!"

Canadian Science

Several years ago, Great Britain funded a study to determine why the head on a man's penis is larger than the shaft. The study took two years and cost over $1.2 million. The study concluded that the reason the head of a man's penis is larger than the shaft was to provide the man with more pleasure during sex.

After the results were published, France decided to conduct their own study on the same subject. They were convinced that the results of the British study were flawed. After three years of research at a cost in excess of $2 million, the French researchers concluded that the head of a man's penis is larger than the shaft to provide the woman with more pleasure during sex.

When the results of the French study were released, Canada decided to conduct their own study. The Canucks didn't really trust British or French studies. So, after nearly three weeks of intensive research and a cost of right around $75, the Canadian study was complete.

They concluded that the reason the head on a man's penis is larger than the shaft is to prevent your hand from flying off and hitting you in the forehead!

The Hitchhiker

One day a man was hiking down an old dirt road when he noticed, down an embankment, a naked man tied to a large tree.

The hiker ran to the man, and while removing his backpack, asked, "What happened to you?"

The tied-up man began to tell him, "I picked up a hitchhiker and a few miles down the road he pulled a gun on me. He told me to pull over and took my car, my money, and all of my clothes. Then he tied me up to this tree."

The hiker unzipped his fly and said, "Boy, this just isn't your day, is it?"

Lesbians Next Door

The lesbians next door bought me a Rolex for my birthday.

I think they misunderstood when I said I wanna watch.

Bad Knees

An elderly retiree wobbled gingerly into an ice cream shop and carefully, slowly climbed up onto a counter stool.

He wheezed for a minute and said, "One chocolate sundae, please."

"Crushed nuts?" asked the server.

"No," the old man answered. "Bad knees."

Grandpa's House

A boy went to his grandfather's house for a week.

On the first night at dinner he found a thick, slimy goo on his plate, so he said to his grandfather "Grandpa, is this plate clean?"

"As clean as cold water can get it," his grandfather answered.

The next morning, the boy fond sticky dried goo on his fork, so he asked his grandpa, "Grandpa, is this fork clean?"

"As clean as cold water can get it," his grandfather answered.

This went on for the rest of the week. On the last day when the boy was leaving the dog was blocking the door, so he said, "Grandpa your dog won't let me through."

His grandfather said to the dog, "Cold Water, go lie down."

City Reporter

A big city reporter traveled to West Virginia to interview some of the backwards hillbillies in a special interest story. He finds a toothless old man sitting in a rocking chair on his porch and decides he'd be the perfect interviewee.

After asking a few introductory questions, the reporter asks, "Can yo tell me about your best day up here on the mountain?"

"Oh, that's easy," said the old man. "That was the day that little girl was lost in the woods. We gathered up a bunch of guys, searched the woods, and found her. And then we all fucked her."

"Oh!" said the reporter. "We can't use that story. How about your second-best day?"

"That was the day my favorite billy goat was lost in the woods. We gathered up a bunch of guys, searched the woods, and found him. And then we all fucked him."

"Wow, hmm, this isn't working. Can you tell me about your worst day on the mountain instead?"

The man spit chewing tobacco on the ground and shook his head, "That would be the day I got lost in the woods."

The Condom

A man calls 911 with an emergency: "Come immediately, my little son has swallowed a condom!"

The dispatcher immediately sent an ambulance.

After five minutes, the same man calls back: "It's ok, I found another one."

Sunday School

Josey wasn't the best pupil at Sunday school. She often fell asleep and one day while she was sleeping, the teacher asked her a question.

"Who is the creator of the universe?"

Joe was sitting next to Josey and decided to poke her with a pin to wake her up.

Josey jumped and yelled, "God almighty!"

The teacher congratulated her.

A little later the teacher asked her another question, "Tell me who is our lord and savior?"

Joe poked Josey again and she yelled out, "Jesus Christ!"

The teacher congratulated her again.

Later on the teacher asked, "What did Eve say to Adam after their 26th child?"

Joe poked Josey again, and she shouted, "If you stick that thing in me again, I'll snap it in half and stick it up your ass!"

The Questions

Q: Why did they make glow in the dark condoms?

A: So gay guys can play Star Wars.

Q: How can you spot the blind guy in a nudist colony?

A: It's not hard.

Q: What are three words you dread the most while making love?

A: "Honey, I'm home."

Q. What do tightrope walking and getting a blowjob from Grandma have in common?

A. You don't look down.

Q: Why do rednecks like having sex doggie style?

A: That way they can both watch wrestling.

Q. What is something nine out of ten people enjoy?

A. Gang rape.

Q. What's the difference between a G-spot and a golf ball?

A. A guy will actually search for a golf ball.

Q. Why was the guitar teacher arrested?

A. For fingering a minor.

Q. What's the difference between a tire and 365 used condoms?

A. One's a Goodyear. The other's a great year.

Q. What's the best part about sex with 28-year-olds?

A. There are twenty of them.

Q. What's the difference between a pregnant woman and a lightbulb?

A. You can unscrew a lightbulb.

Q. What's the difference between a Catholic priest and a zit?

A. A zit will wait until you're twelve before it comes on your face.

Q. What do you call the useless piece of skin on a dick?

A. The man.

Q. What's the difference between your wife and your job?

A. After five years, your job will still suck.

Q. How do you make your girlfriend scream during sex?

A. Call and tell her about it.

The Punishment

One day, a mother and two boys, Timmy and Tommy, were riding in their car on the way to church.

Timmy leaned over, smacked Tommy across the head, and Tommy yelled out "Ouch, you fucking asshole!"

After church, the mom went to talk to the priest.

She said, "Father, my boys just won't stop swearing and I don't know what to do."

The priest thought about it and said, "Well, have you tried smacking them?"

She replied, "No, doesn't the church look down on that?"

The priest said, "Well, yes, but in some cases we'll make an exception."

The next day, the two boys come down for breakfast and the mother asks Tommy what he wants for breakfast.

Tommy said, "Well, gimme some fucking waffles."

The mom immediately backhands Tommy so hard, he flies out of his chair and lands against the door. Shocked and terrified by this, Timmy becomes very quiet.

His mother then turns to him and asks him what he wants for breakfast.

Timmy replied, "Well, you can bet your sweet ass I don't want no fucking waffles!"

The Funeral

A young woman married and had six children. Her husband died. She soon married again and had seven more children. Again, her husband died. But, she remarried and this time had five more children.

Alas, she finally croaked.

Standing before her coffin, the preacher prayed to the Lord above, thanking him for this loving woman who fulfilled his commandment to "Go forth and multiply."

In his final eulogy, he noted, "Thank you Lord, they're finally together."

Leaning over to his neighbor, one mourner asked, "Do you think he means her first, second or third husband?"

The other mourner replied, "I think he means her legs."

The Anniversary

To celebrate their seventh wedding anniversary, a man and his wife spend the weekend at an exclusive golf resort. He is a pretty good golfer, but she only a beginner. When they head down to the golf course after a lavish lunch and a bottle of champagne, they notice a beautiful mansion a couple of hundred yards behind the first hole.

"Let's be extra careful, honey," the husband says, "If we damage that house over there, it'll cost us a fortune."

The wife nods, tees off and - bang! - sends the ball right through the window of the mansion.

"Jesus Christ," the husband says. "I told you to watch out for that house. Alright, let's go up there, apologize and see what the damage is."

They walk up to the house and knock on the door.

"Come on in," a voice in the house says.

The couple open the door and enter the foyer. The living room is a mess. There are pieces of glass all over the floor and a broken bottle near the window. A man sits on the couch.

When the couple enters the room, he gets up and says, "Are you the guys who just broke my window?"

"Um, yeah," the husband replies, "sorry about that."

"Not at all, it's me who has to thank you. I'm a genie and was trapped in that bottle for a thousand years. You've just released me. To show my gratitude, I'm allowed to grant each of you a wish. But - I'll require one favor in return."

"Really? That's great!" the husband says. "I want a million dollars a year for the rest of my life." "

"No problem. That's the least I can do. And you, what do you want?" the genie asks, looking at the wife.

"I want a house in every country of the world," the wife says.

The genie smiles, "Consider it done."

"And what's this favor we must grant in return, genie?" the husband asks.

"Well, since I've been trapped in that stupid bottle for the last thousand years, I haven't had sex with a woman for a very long time. My wish is to sleep with your wife."

The husband scratches his head, looks at the wife and says, "Well, we did get a lot of money and all these houses, honey. So I guess I'm fine if it's alright with you."

The genie and the wife disappear in a room upstairs and make love for an hour, while the husband stays in the living room.

When they are done, the genie rolls over, looks at the wife and asks, "How old exactly is your husband?"

"Thirty-one," she replies.

"And he still believes in genies? That's amazing!"

The Train Tracks

A man walks into a bar with a huge grin on his face.

"What are you so happy about?" asks the bartender.

"Well, I live by the railway and on my way home last night, I noticed a woman tied to the tracks. I cut her free and we shagged all night!"

"Wow, that's lucky! Did you get a blow job?" asks the bartender.

"No," he says, "I never found the head."

The Camping Trip

Little gay Johnny asks Billy, "If you went camping and woke up with a condom in your butt, would you tell anyone?

Billy says, "No way, that'd be embarrassing".

Johnny then asks, "Wanna go camping?"

The Prostitute

A prostitute walks into the police station and declares, "I was raped!"

The desk officer takes down her information and asks, "So when did you realize you were raped?"

She replied, "When the check bounced!"

The Lobsterman

After a day fishing in the ocean, a fisherman is walking from the pier carrying two lobsters in a bucket. He is approached by the Game Warden who asks to see his fishing license.

The fisherman says to the warden, "I did not catch these lobsters, they are my pets. Everyday I come down to the water and whistle, and these lobster jump out and I take them for a walk only to return them at the end of the day."

The warden, not believing him, reminds him that it is illegal to fish without a license.

The fisherman turns to the warden and says, "If you don't believe me then watch," as he throws the lobsters back into the water.

The warden says, "Now whistle to your lobster and show me that they will come out of the water."

The fisherman turns to the warden and says, "What lobster?"

The Genie

A guy is walking along the shoreline at the beach. A wave deposits a bottle on the beach right in front of him. He picks up a bottle, pulls the cork, and out comes the Genie to give him one wish.

"Hmmm," the man says thoughtfully, "Can you bring peace to the Middle East?"

The Genie pales, and says, "Master, these people have been at war since time began. It is their nature, woven into the very fabric of their lives. What you ask is totally impossible. It is probably the only wish I cannot grant you. Ask for anything else and I will make it happen."

"Okay", the guy says. "Tomorrow morning have my wife awaken me, with the best blowjob I've ever had, on her own, without my begging and pleading - just because she likes it, because she wants to, and because it turns her on."

The Genie shakes his head and says, "So, peace in the Middle East, you say?"

The Challenge

I stopped a girl in the street last night and handed her a rape alarm and some pepper spray.

She looked confused and said, "What are these for?"

I started unbuttoning my jeans and replied, "I like a challenge."

The Kinky Man

A man says to his wife, "I've always wanted to try kinky sex, how about I blow my load in your ear?"

The wife replies, "No way, I might go deaf!"

To which the man replies, "I've been shooting my wad in your mouth for the last five years and you're still talking, aren't you?"

The Park Bench

Two nuns are sitting on a park bench. A man in a trench coat runs up and flashes them. The first nun has a stroke.

The second nun tried but she couldn't reach it in time.

The Pirate

A pirate walks into a bar with a ship's steering wheel stuck to the front of his pants.

The bartender asks, "Hey, doesn't that hurt?"

The pirate growls, "Aye, it's drivin' me nuts."

We hope you've enjoyed **World's Dirtiest Jokes** as much as we did creating it! Please take the time to write a five-star Amazon review.

Printed in Great Britain
by Amazon

43280839R00155